I0601572

This Means War

Benna Bos

2026

Bywater Books

Copyright 2026 Benna Bos

All rights reserved. No part of this book may be
reproduced, stored in a retrieval system, or transmitted
in any form or by any means, without prior permission
in writing from the publisher.

Print ISBN: 978-1-61294-331-2

Bywater Books First Edition: February 2026

Printed in the United States of America on acid-free paper.

Cover designer: TreeHouse Studio

Bywater Books
PO Box 3671
Ann Arbor MI 48106-3671

www.bywaterbooks.com

This is a work of fiction. Names, characters, places,
and incidents are the product of the author's imagination
or are used fictitiously. Any resemblance to actual events,
locales, or persons living or dead is fictionalized.

To Jim and Stephanie, who both helped me explore many spooky ghost towns.

MAP OF THEIA

To Cemetery
Meyer Mansion
Blacksmith
Corral
Proposed
Historic Park
Saddlery
Warsaw Saloon
Laundry
General Store
Hotel
Molly's Cabin
The Primrose
Bothwood Mansion
The Shop (old Assay Office)
Bachelors' Quarters
Jail
Town Hall
The Oasis

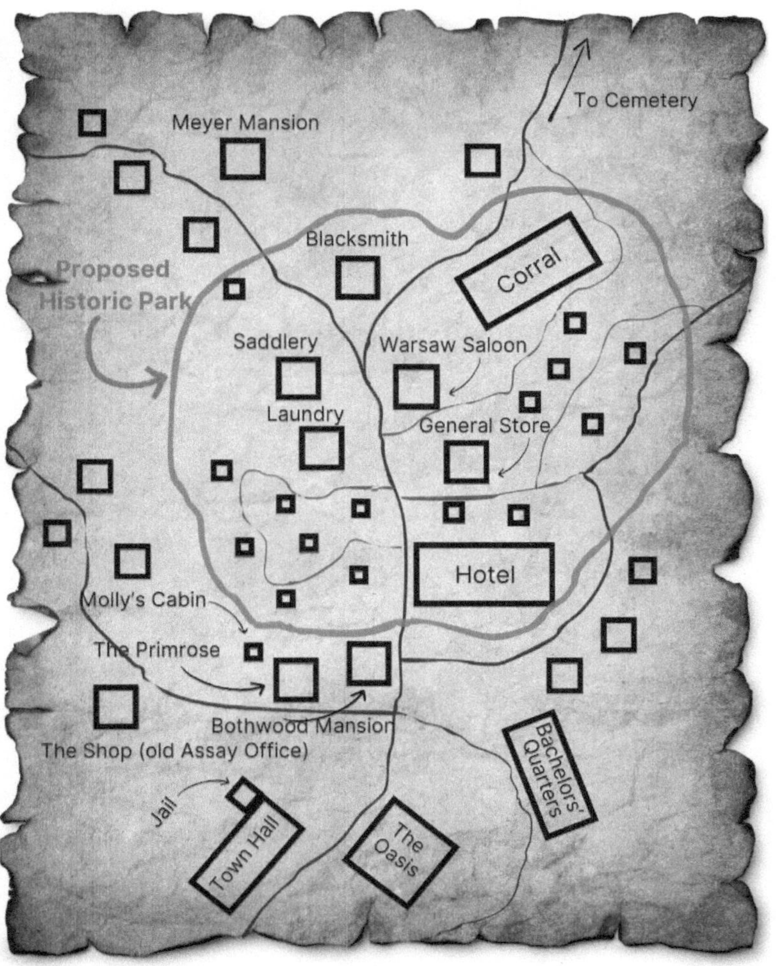

Chapter One

Molly wove her fingers through the cold metal of the ugly gate standing between the old road and the legendary saloon. Twenty yards beyond the fence, the slatted, swinging doors winked at her. Their hinges, long since rusted, left them permanently stuck in mid-motion, frozen in time, like the saloon itself. That iconic entrance beckoned her to bring her people inside for her greatest story. But she could not reach it.

Instead of telling the best joke on her tour, one that usually resulted in extra tips, all that came out of Molly's mouth was, "What the hell?"

Mary, the matriarch of the large family that were her guests this afternoon, tapped her shoulder. "Is something wrong, Molly?"

Unable to wrap her head around what was happening, Molly turned to Mary with a classic tour guide smile plastered on her face. "Would you mind taking everyone across the street?" She pointed to the other side of the rutted dirt path that was barely wide enough for any modern vehicle. "There's a great view of the mountains over there, and it's the perfect place to take group photos. I'll join you in just a minute."

Mary's concerned gaze lingered over the fence for a moment before she turned to round up the tour group with a forceful voice. "All right, everyone, follow me."

Molly moved away from the group, following the fence around toward the side of the property. But there was no break, no opening, no sign reading, "just kidding, come on in!"

Just as the weight of despair was dropping down on her with force, her eye caught movement. She pressed herself against the cold metal and zeroed in on it. A few seconds later, it happened again. She could swear she saw an elbow. Yes, it was definitely an elbow peeking out from the back of the building. Molly shouted toward it. "Hey! Hey!"

A man's head, covered with a blue ball cap, appeared beside the splintered wood siding of the building. "Hello?"

"Hey! Yeah, hey!" Molly waved her arms wildly. He was no more than twenty feet away, but her eagerness to be addressed overrode any common sense.

The man loped toward her slowly. "Hi. What's up?"

"What's with the fence?"

He shrugged. "I didn't put it up."

"It literally wasn't here yesterday."

He shrugged again. "It was here when I got on site a couple of hours ago."

"Well, what's going on? Why are you here? Why is this fence here?" The questions popped out of her, each one spoken in a slightly higher tone than the one before. Then she turned, her voice deeper, harder. "You know this is a protected site, right? You can't just put up a modern fence in the middle of a ghost town. You know that, right?"

That Theia was in the early application stages of potentially becoming a protected historic site was not relevant at that moment. Molly was willing to bend the truth and use scare tactics if it got her answers.

But the man seemed immune to her threats. He held up his hands and took a step back. "Look, lady, I don't call the shots here. I was hired to make an estimate, and that's all."

Molly grasped onto that tiny bit of information. "An estimate for what?"

The guy turned his head to the side, briefly flashing his gaze back to the spot he'd abandoned when she called out to him. "I don't think it's my place to talk about this with you. You should talk to the new owner."

"New owner?"

"Yeah." He moved away faster now. "I gotta go."

"Wait! Who's the new owner?"

He didn't answer. Instead, he slipped around the side of the building, safe behind the stupid fence.

Molly's head dropped back, and she released a loud sigh. This day had turned to shit fast, but this wasn't just about today. It was about Theia. This place was special, and someone was clearly trying to destroy it.

The Oasis was crowded, indicating that the tourist season had truly arrived with the warm late-spring weather. Through the windows, Molly could see that every table in the main part of the restaurant was packed, and an organized line of patrons waited outside the front door.

Molly moved toward the building's back entrance. The modest pine covered with peeling red paint didn't hold the same welcome as the well-polished oak front door that greeted the restaurant's customers on the other side. Since this back entrance led to Theia's only bar, it was well used by the locals. She pulled it open, the squeak of the old hinges so familiar they felt like the bark of a well-loved dog.

Not two seconds after she stepped into the tiny, dim space, a real dog jumped up, its front paws landing above her knee. Molly leaned down to pat her head. "Hey, Rosie. How are you tonight, sweetheart?"

The little dog wagged her tail and attempted to lick Molly's wrist before jumping down and following Molly's path across the wood floor to the sturdy bar. The gorgeous soul behind it smiled. "Hey there."

Molly scooped Rosie up, dropped onto a barstool, and tucked the pup into her lap. "Hey."

Etta grabbed a bottle from the back of the bar and a glass from the rack above it, and poured. "You look like you had a rough day. Difficult tour group?"

"They were fine." Molly took the offered glass of whiskey from her best friend. "But I've got a big problem. We all do."

Etta raised one eyebrow. "Sounds intriguing." She grabbed two beers with one hand and passed them to Dale and Hines, who were also sitting at the bar, with one empty seat between them and Molly. The other two of the six seats were occupied by Jeff and Lana who, based on their attire, had just gotten off shift at the attached restaurant.

"Someone bought the saloon," Molly said.

"We heard." Etta dropped a half-dozen ice cubes in a glass and started mixing a drink. "Not only the saloon, but all of Stan's property."

"Yeah," Dale said, lifting his beer. "Word's all over town."

Molly twisted on the stool to look at him. "What did you hear?"

Dale twirled the neck of his beer bottle. "Old man Stan sold everything he had to some rich chick from California."

The words "rich chick from California" slid up Molly's spine like icicles. She'd had her life destroyed by one of those. Fingers of resentment wound around her gut. Not again.

Jeff piped up from the other side of Molly. "No way. He was so into being the largest landowner in Theia. He'd never sell out."

It was a big deal. Theia had once been a thriving mining town. But when the gold dried up, the town was abandoned. It had been nothing more than rotting buildings sitting alone on the valley floor for over a hundred years until a handful of Montanans moved back. The new residents were able to provide food and lodging to tourists who came to see the original town site and relive its Wild West legends.

The core of the town remained the same. The dilapidated old buildings that only hinted at what they once were fascinated tourists who drove twenty miles off the main highway through winding hills and lonely ranches to walk among them and imagine what the town was like in its heyday. The residents who'd fixed up the more manageable homes on the perimeter made their living off those tourists and their welcome dollars. That's why Molly and a handful of others were trying to get the state to designate Theia as a historic site, to prevent exactly what had just happened.

Stan may not have been on the preservation committee, but someone who had his ear certainly was, and he'd shown nothing but support for their plans. Could he really have been swayed by cold, hard cash?

Etta slapped her hand on the bar. "He told me he was going to leave everything he owned, except the house he lives in, to the state in his will so they could turn it into a historic park. He always promised that he would own it until the day he went to his grave."

He'd told Molly that, too. Her plans to have a state park in the center of town hinged on Stan's cooperation. Everything she'd been working toward for years was hanging in the balance. Her stomach churned.

"Apparently he changed his mind," Dale said.

Molly leaned toward Dale. "Who did he sell to?"

Dale shrugged. "Like I said, some rich chick from California. That's all I know."

Etta propped her elbows on the bar. "And who did you hear that from?"

"Stan. I ran into him at the grocery store in Bozeman yesterday. He said this woman called him out of the blue and offered him whatever he wanted for his properties, and especially the Warsaw Saloon. He told her he wouldn't give it up for less than a million dollars, and she offered him a million dollars. Can you believe that?"

"Wait, what?!" at least three people in the bar said at once. Molly might have been one of them.

"Yep. He got a million freaking dollars for a bunch of falling-apart old buildings." Dale hefted his beer and took a long swig.

Molly pulled in a deep breath. Something was off. Way off. That land wasn't worth one quarter of that amount, and the old buildings were only worth what you could get in scrap prices. Their value lay in the history they stored within. "Who's the buyer?"

Dale shrugged again. "I told you—"

"Yeah. Some chick from California." Molly tried to curb her impatience. "Did he say a name?"

"Nope."

Etta leaned toward Dale, grabbed his beer away from him and glared at him. "What did he say about her?"

Dale took a painfully long time to answer. He swiped a hand through his thick sandy hair, sat back on the barstool, and rubbed his palms over his jean-covered thighs. "I know she's staying at the Primrose."

Molly hadn't moved so quickly in years. She shot off the barstool and ran out the door in a matter of seconds.

Chapter Two

Molly burst through the door of her parents' bed-and-breakfast as if the hounds of hell were on her heels. Her mother had arranged the front room with vintage furniture she claimed was very close to what would have been there when it was freshly built for the Moore family to live in back in 1887.

Molly nearly tripped over a settee as she charged through the room and headed toward the kitchen. She wasn't sure if she'd find her parents there, but even if they weren't in the kitchen, at least one of them would be in the airy, window-lined office adjacent to it.

It was after dinnertime, and Janet and Jeb Green would be ensuring the comfort of all their overnight guests. So at least one of them had to be in that part of the house preparing tea and cookies or checking the computer for the details they needed for the next morning.

She shoved open the swinging, saloon-style doors and found them both there, her mother brewing a batch of tea and her father elbow deep in dish soap bubbles.

"Mom, Dad." Even to her own ears she sounded winded and desperate, which is exactly what she was.

"Hi, honey." Her mother's voice was as soft and sweet as always.

Molly attempted to temper her volume so guests wouldn't

hear her panicked holler. "What's going on?"

Her father wiped his hands on a towel and approached her. "Everything's good here. Are you all right, dear?"

"No. I'm not okay." She dropped her voice another register before speaking again. "Do you have a guest here that bought half of Theia, including the Warsaw Saloon?"

Her parents exchanged a suspiciously knowing glance.

Her father's voice was deep, smooth, and way too calm. "There's a guest here who expressed that she may have purchased Stan's buildings."

"Dad. Do not play with me. Tell me everything you know."

Her father placed a gentle hand on her shoulder. "Well, honey. I can't tell you everything."

"Meaning the town council already knows about this?"

"Yes. There will be a discussion at the public meeting tomorrow. So you, along with the rest of the town, will find out everything then."

Betrayal bloomed in Molly's gut. She knew her father took his role on the town council seriously. But this was something that was imperative to the survival of the entire town, and that included her livelihood. Not to mention that he knew full well she had been working tirelessly for the historic preservation status. If anything was changed significantly, it could threaten that. How could he not tell her?

"What about the historic preservation committee, Dad? Isn't the council going to ask our opinion? You all approved our plans."

"We did. And we're not making any decisions tomorrow, just getting information. From there, everyone, including the committee, can decide how we want to proceed."

"Do you really have a choice?" her mother asked.

Jeb turned to look at his wife. "What do you mean?"

"I mean, it's all private property. If Stan sold it, can't the new owner do what they want with it? The historic designation hasn't gone through yet."

Molly felt her heart racing. She wanted to tell her mother that, yes, she was correct. That was precisely what could happen. But she was struggling to breathe. Hearing it laid out like that was wreaking havoc on her nervous system.

Her father took a moment to frown before answering. "Technically, yes. But the new owner has asked to present her ideas at a town meeting. She said she wants to have buy-in. It felt very genuine to me."

Jeb Green was not a naïve man. He did everything with an overabundance of optimism, but also with a lot of analysis. He didn't have Molly's background with those buildings. He probably couldn't even name every building that Stan had once owned. Molly could. She not only knew the common name and original owner, but could pull up a visual of what it looked like right now. And in her file she had a drawing of each building with the needed repairs identified on each one.

She knew those buildings better than anyone other than Stan himself. She thought about heading straight to Stan's house and talking to him directly. But if he was willing to sell for a million dollars, there might be no reasoning with him. Maybe she'd have better luck with the buyer.

"I need a name."

Her mother turned to her father. "Jeb, she's going to find out tomorrow anyway. Plus half the guests here already know. You may as well just tell her."

"Why do the guests know?"

Her mother scratched her chin. "She's a little famous. Famous-ish. I mean she should be famous. But since we live in a misogynistic culture—"

"Mom. Who is she?"

"Persephone Milan."

Jeb shot Janet a stern look. She merely shrugged.

Molly must have looked like a statue standing there in front of her parents with her brain spinning out of control. Persephone Milan. It couldn't be.

Her mother moved forward and placed a hand on Molly's other shoulder. She apparently took her silence as ignorance. "She's the ex-wife of Greg Milan."

Molly knew exactly who she was. Molly had been in journalism before ruining her career and running to Theia though her parents kept talking as if this was all news to her.

"I know you know that name. His company is the kind everyone wishes they'd bought stock in back in the day," her father said. "Except while we all know his name, what we didn't know until the very public divorce is that she played a major role in helping him build his empire. She stayed in the shadows the whole time."

"More like was forced into the shadows the way I heard it. Anyway, surely you heard about the divorce, Molly. It was all over the news."

Molly nodded slowly. It couldn't be.

"So, yeah. She bought all of Stan's property." Her mother snapped her fingers. "Just like that. And she's in town to work out the details."

Molly finally found her voice. "But why? Why did she do that? Why is she here?"

Her parents shrugged in sync.

"You'd have to ask her," her mother said.

"I will. What room is she in?"

"The Georgette."

"Janet!" Her father looked aghast.

Janet turned toward Jeb. "What? She'd just wait until we were serving tea and look on the computer anyway. What's the point in keeping it from her? Speaking of tea." Her mother looked at her watch. "The guests are probably gathering now. We need to get going. Molly, grab the cookies."

Molly did as she was told. She picked up the plate piled high with cookies and followed her parents into the sitting room. Her mother was right. Guests were already starting to file in, perching on the replica furniture, looking excited and ready for the stories her parents would be telling by the light of the fireplace.

As the great-great-grandchild of the town's last mayor before the mine went belly-up, her father was a bit of a local celebrity. And he used that to make the Primrose worth every dollar to the people who skipped the cheap rentals and wanted a full, immersive experience.

As soon as Jeb was completely engaged with the guests and Janet had ducked back into the kitchen to get more cookies, Molly slipped out and up the back stairway.

When she reached the third floor, she turned down the hall and practically sprinted to the room at the end. It was the largest of the guest rooms, and the only one with an en suite bathroom. Janet had lovingly decorated it in rose and gold with matching oak pieces. It was well worth the top dollar they were getting for renting it to their guests.

Molly had helped her mother paint the words "The Georgette" in flowing script on the door. Now she slammed her knuckles below those words. There was a long beat before a muffled voice from inside answered. A few moments later, the door swung open.

Dark, rich curls draped down bare shoulders. A silky summer dress hung over curves Molly remembered well. And planted in wedge sandals, legs that went on forever with smooth brown skin that Molly could still taste on her tongue.

Chapter Three

Seph Cosmo had been a fevered college dream that came true one magical night before graduation.

Molly had minored in history, and that was Seph's major, so they shared classes occasionally at UC Berkeley. Every semester where they shared the same space felt like the building crescendo of an erotic novel. At a party, the night before graduation, it all came crashing down in a torrential rainstorm of heat, lust, and sex.

For a decade they'd lived apart. Seph as Persephone Milan, wife of the tech genius, and Molly as a failed journalist holed up in a ghost town giving tours. Now here they both were, face to face again.

"Molly Green?"

"Yep. It's me."

Seph laughed. Her long, kissable neck vibrated at Molly's eye level. Molly swallowed hard and tried to grasp onto her anger. "Wow. I guess I should have known you'd show up sooner or later."

Seph stepped back and waved a hand toward the room. Molly moved in cautiously, and Seph shut the door behind her. "I knew you were from Theia, and I deduced once I got to the Primrose that you're Janet and Jeb's daughter. But I didn't realize you'd moved back home."

"And you got married to the tech bro you were dating in college. Hence the last name."

Seph glided over to the set of chairs Molly's mother had arranged by the window and sat down in one. Molly slid into the other, hands pressed to her knees.

"I did. And now I'm divorced, thank god. It's Seph Cosmo again."

Molly leaned toward Seph. "I heard you got more than a name change in the divorce."

"I earned that money." Seph looked Molly up and down, her eyes tracking Molly's body slowly, roaming from one sensuous place to the next with intention. "What about you? You were studying journalism in school, right?"

"I worked in the field for a while. And then I . . ." Molly paused. She didn't come here to catch up, and confessing all the life mistakes that led to them both being here in this moment wasn't going to help her in the conversation to come. "I write books actually."

"Yes! I know." Seph jumped up and moved quickly to a leather suitcase perched on the rack near the bed. She pulled out one of Molly's books on Theia and held it up. "You wrote this."

"Yeah. That's the first. Number four will be coming out soon." If she ever finished writing it.

"My tour guide gave it to me."

That brought the real issue back into the room like an elephant on full stomp mode. "Your tour guide?"

"Shannon McGregor. Do you know her? She gives great tours of Theia."

Molly could feel the anger moving through her like a living thing. Not only was this woman trying to ruin her career, but she had decided to do it while on a tour with Molly's main rival. "Oh, I know Shannon. So you went on one of her hackneyed tours and decided to buy the town, huh?"

Seph looked down at the book again for a brief moment

before turning her gaze back to Molly. "That's pretty much how it went, yeah."

Molly stepped toward Seph. "Give it back."

Seph stared at her as if she were speaking a different language. "What? The book?"

"No. The town and the saloon. Give it all back to Stan."

Seph placed the book on top of her suitcase and rolled her shoulders. "No. I've got plans."

Molly tapped her foot on the floor. It echoed back at her. "I have plans for it, too."

"But you don't own it. How could you have plans for something you don't own?"

Molly could feel that question flow through her like a wave of fire. She took a deep breath and tried to remember that she and Seph were coming at this from different angles. "The town has a historic preservation committee. We've created a master plan that includes every one of the buildings you bought. We've been working on this for years."

"So, tell me about the plans?"

Molly nodded. "I can do that. We can talk through what we're going to do."

"What you *want* to do."

Molly's teeth gnashed together. "What we're *going* to do."

Seph cocked her head to one side. It would have been adorable if it weren't for the threatening gleam in her eye. "As the new owner of eleven properties, I'm happy to discuss your plans with an open mind."

"Stan owned ten intact buildings."

"Yep. I also bought the Bothwood mansion."

Molly focused on her breathing. That was not ideal, but it was less of a concern at the moment because it was outside of the planned park. "How about we meet after breakfast in the great room downstairs? I'll bring the plans."

"Perfect." Seph cocked up one eyebrow. "I'll bring *my* plans."

Molly's jaw dropped. She could feel it happen, and she had to quickly snap her jaw shut. "When, exactly, did you buy the property?"

"The deal went through last week, but I called Stan a month ago. I asked him to keep it under wraps until it was all done. That gave my architect lots of time to plan. Good thing, too, because I'm getting started on the renovations right away."

The giant fence flashed through Molly's mind and sparked her anger, allowing it to eclipse the confusion and awe she'd been temporarily mired in. "Yeah. I saw the fence around the Warsaw."

"The Warsaw and my house are first. I'm leaving the other nine buildings until next summer. So." She shrugged. "Maybe we can negotiate."

Molly stared at Seph with contempt. She'd walked into this town with her own plans. Getting her to listen to anyone was going to be difficult. But Molly had to try. She let her mother's oft-quoted words about catching flies with honey flow through her.

"I look forward to having a productive conversation tomorrow." Molly held out her hand.

"See you then." Seph shook her hand, and Molly could swear that the contact burned.

Molly pushed her way through the door, two massive ring binders cradled in her arms. Seph sat opposite Jeb and Janet Green. The three of them were enjoying tea and nibbling on cookies. Seph was in mid-laugh, her head thrown back, her dark hair dropping down her back like moss hanging from a willow in an elegant and mysterious forest, when she turned her head to peer at Molly.

"Hi, honey," Janet said. "We were talking about what a coincidence it is that you and Persephone went to the same university at the same time."

Molly glared at Seph, who grinned back at her.

"Yeah. We did." Molly marched into the room and dropped her binders on the coffee table that sat between Seph and her parents. "Are you ready to talk about Theia?"

"I remember your graduation," Janet said, flashing Seph a massive grin.

Seph frowned and turned to Molly. "Yes. Let's jump on in."

If Janet was offended by the abrupt change of subject, she didn't mention it.

Molly stood in front of the seat beside Seph, the one she needed to take, but she wasn't quite ready to be that close yet. She scanned the area around Seph and saw nothing. "I thought you were bringing blueprints?"

Seph pulled a tablet out of the side of the settee. "I have them here." She nodded toward the load Molly had placed on the table. "But I want to see yours first."

Molly gave in to the inevitable and dropped into the spot beside Seph. "Okay." She reached for the first binder and flopped open the cover. "Let's start with the master plan for Theia."

"Yes. Let's." Seph's smile was smug.

Molly glanced over at her parents. Her mother leaned over, elbows on her knees, teacup cradled in her hands. Her father leaned back into the cushions of the cream-colored love seat, his arm slung over the back behind Janet.

"The historic preservation committee, with the approval of the town council, have been working on a master plan to create a historic park in the center of town. Have you ever been to the ghost town park that sits on the edge of West Yellowstone?"

Seph nodded. "Actually, yes. I went there with my cousin a few years back."

"Great! Then you can see the vision. We want to do something very similar here. That one has less than half the original buildings we have in Theia. So ours would be larger, and Theia has a longer and richer history, which we'll showcase in the core of the ghost town that is preserved as a historic park." Molly turned the laminated pages of her binder until she reached a two-page spread. She spun the binder so Seph could see the illustration better. With her finger, she circled the area that housed twenty-two decrepit buildings, ten of which Seph now owned. "We'll put a fence around it."

"I thought you hated fences."

"What?"

Seph flashed a glance at Jeb. "I heard it was the fence around the Warsaw that had you so worked up yesterday."

"This would be a cute picket fence. Not the same. Anyway, the purpose of it is simply to control traffic and allow the park to have open and closed times. We could also charge for special events, putting the money into a preservation fund."

"I see. So you want to fence it and charge. Go on."

Seph's arrogant tone as she purposely misrepresented what Molly said made Molly swell with resentment. Molly took a moment to summon every shred of patience she had. Fortunately, her audience waited. When she was ready, she took in a deep breath, bringing the scent of Seph's perfume in—sweet, floral, and utterly perfect for the elegant woman beside her.

Molly shook that off. "The rest of the buildings, outside the historic park, can continue to be renovated for modern use, as they have been. This would include the Bothwood mansion which you bought."

Molly thought Seph would be grateful for this concession. Instead, she just grunted.

"Anyway. The historic park stays as it is."

"As it is? That seems unsafe at best."

"Let me rephrase. We will ensure that the buildings are renovated in ways to make them safe for entry. But we are not looking to paint them up and make them shiny. We're trying to preserve the ghost town aesthetic in this part of town. If people want to see a building returned to its original glory and beyond, they can visit the town hall, the Primrose, the Oasis. If they want to experience a ghost town and that unique feel of walking through the past in a place that has been left to time, they will go into the ghost town historic park. You get the picture?"

"I do."

"So?"

Seph leaned back, folding her arms over her chest. "It's one way to do it."

"It's the way the entire town has agreed upon."

Seph raised an eyebrow. "The entire town?"

"Yeah."

Seph moved her gaze over to Jeb and Janet. When Molly followed suit and looked at her parents, they were both staring down at their hands.

"The city council approved the historic preservation plan."

"What about the property owners?"

Molly moved her first binder aside and pulled out the second one. She flipped open the cover, which landed with a thud on the other binder. "This is the paperwork that is currently under consideration for historic preservation. Every property owner for the buildings in the designated part of town—Stan, my dad, and three others—signed it, saying they agreed to the plans." Molly tapped her finger on the plastic sheet protector covering the page with the signatures. "They all also agree to deed the property to the state as part of the historic park either after designation or upon their death."

Seph tapped her chin with one well-manicured finger. "But it's currently sitting in an inbox at a government agency, right?"

"I suppose."

"And it's not accurate anymore." Seph moved that finger and dropped it right on Stan's signature. "Because now I own nearly half the buildings listed."

Molly had to rip her eyes away from Seph to glance over at her parents. They weren't staring into the depths of their teacups anymore. They were both looking right at Seph. Finally, the Greens were all on the same page.

"So, can we see your plans?" Molly asked.

Seph didn't verbally respond. She pressed the button on her tablet and started to swipe through it until, seemingly satisfied, she placed it on top of the signature page. "Okay. So here's my vision." She gestured over a picture that appeared to have been taken by a drone. "These buildings are all original cabins." Seph tapped at each of six buildings on the image with her bright blue fingernail. "And they are in varying states of rough shape. Right now it's not safe to enter four of the six of them."

Molly couldn't argue with that assessment. She actually thought that none of the six were safe. But shoring them up was already part of the preservation plans. And she and the committee had been working to raise money for that. Still, she kept her mouth shut and waited to see what else Seph had to say.

"I want to rebuild them."

Molly and her parents reacted at the same time, practically shouting over one another. "Rebuild?"

"Yeah. We'll level them and rebuild them so they look exactly like they would have back in the day." Seph smiled like this was the best idea ever.

Molly's shout could not be controlled. "That's a terrible idea!"

Seph frowned. "Why?"

Molly wasn't even sure where to start. She was dumbfounded. This woman had majored in history for crying out loud! How could she not see how destructive her plan was?

Jeb cleared his throat. "We would prefer to preserve the original building. To rebuild is simply to create a replica."

Janet reached over the table to place a gentle hand over Seph's. "You know, like how they re-created Old Faithful at that theme park. Not the same as the real thing."

Seph nodded. "Okay. I hear what you're saying. But let me tell you the rest of the plans before we get into details."

"Good idea," Jeb said.

"I'm not only going to renovate the buildings I own. I plan to fix up all twenty-two buildings. The focus for tourists will be the commercial buildings—the hotel, store, blacksmith shop, corral, laundry, saddlery, and of course the saloon. Those buildings will feature tours and historic demonstrations. The cabins ringing the commercial buildings will be open for people to see, but more like on your own peek and looks, ya know."

"So, are you going to charge admission?" Janet asked.

Molly shook her head. "Wait. Back up. How you are going to do this with buildings that other people own?"

Seph gestured toward Janet with her open palm. "To answer your question, I plan to have it all open for free. What people will pay for is their meals, drinks, private tours, etc. That way, the people who make their living here are the focus of the economics. I'll fund the restoration myself."

Molly's own question withered beneath that explanation. It was generous as hell, and despite the many flaws already showing through Seph's plans like expanding rust spots, this one piece could win a lot of people over.

No one was getting rich off the tourist trade in Theia. They were here out of a love for the place. Most of them had at least one other gig, aside from their store, restaurant, or bed-and-breakfast, to keep them living here. When she'd first moved back to Theia, Molly barely made gas and grocery money giving tours as often as she could drum up business for them over the duration of the short tourist season.

Things were different for her now. Her books and speaking engagements had made her comfortable, and because of their success she conducted tours only two to three times a week and charged four times as much for them. That left a hole for others to give tours more often at cheaper rates. She was happy to have opened up that revenue stream. She was not, however, pleased that the independently wealthy hobbyist from Bozeman, Shannon McGregor, had been the one to step into that space and provide tours as expensive and infrequent as hers. And that was, of course, who Seph had chosen to take her tour with. That was who had started this whole mess.

Molly pushed aside her angst toward Shannon and focused on what Seph was saying. "As for the other owners, I plan to buy out those who will let me."

"I'm sorry," Jeb said. "I'd never sell the three cabins and the corral I own. They're part of my family legacy."

Seph held out her hand, palm up, like she was making an offering. "I understand completely. Then I will ask you to enter into a contract with me that allows me to renovate those spaces free of charge."

Jeb examined her for a moment, his eyes roaming over her face as if he were assessing her. "First, let me say, that is an incredibly generous offer. However, I don't want those buildings torn down and rebuilt. I don't want that to happen to any of them. And I'm quite certain the rest of the town doesn't either."

Molly straightened her spine. The Greens would be a united front Seph couldn't break through. She'd never even make it to the city hall meeting at this rate.

Seph dropped back against the delicate settee, and Molly felt it move a fraction of an inch across the hardwood floor. "I see I may have made a bit of an error in my plans. I had intended to keep the commercial buildings in place and restore them, new boards where the old ones were rotted, replace windows, shore up the foundations, that kind of thing. But those buildings are pretty sturdy to begin with. The cabins didn't seem worth renovating. It would be cheaper to rebuild them. Plus, I had this whole idea of making them look like they would have back then."

Janet set her teacup down beside Seph's tablet, calling everyone's attention to her. "You could fix them up as they stand and still place original furniture in them. Some of the old bed frames and chests are still in the buildings. And there's a salvage yard between here and Bozeman that has a lot of treasures from Theia as well. Your vision isn't all the way off; it just needs tweaking."

Molly couldn't agree with that. She didn't want Seph to tweak her plan. She wanted to stick to the plan the committee had worked so hard on. They would create a state historic park, not some commercial playground owned by a rich California interloper. Everything about this tasted wrong on Molly's tongue.

Seph smiled wide. "I tell you what. I'm going to take a fresh look at things." She scooped up her tablet and stood. "And I'll talk to my people. I'll have an altered plan at the town hall meeting tomorrow."

Molly stood as well. "Wait."

Seph cocked her head. "Yes."

"I want to propose a plan for you to consider."

"Okay."

"Don't do any of this." She gestured to the tablet. "Just give the property back and let us continue with *our* plans. Go find a new project."

Seph's jaw tightened. Her gaze bored into Molly. Her lips pressed together so hard they practically disappeared. "No."

"No? Just no?"

"No."

Anger and frustration froze Molly's brain. Apparently, her parents were also struck incapable of speech. Hearing no retort, Seph spun on her heel and marched off toward the stairs.

Molly wasn't certain if she said aloud what came out of her mouth next or not. "This means war."

Chapter Four

"It's a town council meeting. How pretty do you have to look?" Molly called toward the bathroom.

Rosie gave a little whine. Etta kicked the door open and shouted back, "You know I'm working on getting Jenny Fine to realize that I'm her dream girl. Don't even play with me."

Molly laughed. The famous queer romance novelist had moved to town last year for a "quieter life," and Etta was bound and determined to show her there was some spice in Theia.

Molly had only had a few conversations with Jenny, but she felt a kinship. They were both residents who made their core income on writing. Though in Molly's case, her writing career, like the living of most of the other residents in town, depended on Theia. She liked that Jenny Fine would be at the meeting, but they didn't have the same thing at stake.

"She does write a killer age-gap romance." Molly was not entirely opposed to encouraging Etta's crush. Etta deserved a love story. And if Jenny liked younger women as the characters in her books did, Molly couldn't imagine a better target for her affections than Etta.

"Damn right she does." Etta emerged from the bathroom, looking truly stunning. She scooped Rosie up and sat on the couch opposite Molly's favorite chair.

The little cabin was small, but was just right for Molly.

Perched in the far corner of her parents' large yard, it had every-thing she needed: a sitting room, small kitchen, and a bedroom big enough for a bed and a dresser. Everything else, like laun-dry or entertaining space, she could go to the Primrose for. "So what's the plan?"

"When the public comment period starts, we stir up the crowd. We talk about hoarding history, ruining the potential historic designation, and turning Theia into Kekker. No one here wants to be Kekker."

That one six-letter word was a weapon Molly knew she could wield in this fight. The town of Kekker had once been like Theia, an abandoned ghost town with a rich history. Its location, a handful of miles from the main road leading to Billings, had made it a popular tourist site until a real estate developer bought it all up and turned it into a kitschy ghost town theme park. The renovations were so bad the state historical society wouldn't touch it with a ten-foot pole, and the town was so garish that not even the tourists were into it. It was dried up again, only now it wasn't worth getting out of the car to see, much less driving off the beaten path for.

Etta cocked her head. "What makes you think it will be like that?"

"She's already put up a fence around the Warsaw. She's plan-ning to renovate it." Molly made air quotes with her fingers as Etta frowned. "And she told my parents and me that she plans to tear down and rebuild the cabins she bought off Stan."

"Really?"

"Yes, really. We have to demand that Seph return the prop-erty to Stan or donate it to the state."

"Seph?"

"Persephone. Whatever."

"Okay. So after we demand that, then what?"

"Then everyone gets behind me, and we all say the same thing, and the town council has no choice but to stop her."

"Stop her how?"

"They can get her construction permits revoked."

Etta chewed on her bottom lip. "So, what is Persephone's proposal exactly?"

"Like I said, rebuild the cabins. In fact, she wants to rebuild all the cabins, even the ones that don't belong to her, and make them *replicas* of what they used to be. Then she wants to renovate the commercial buildings and make them operating businesses."

"Hmmm."

"That's all you have to say?"

Etta shrugged. "It sounds bad. I mean, the rebuilding part, for sure. But the businesses thing . . . I don't know. Let's go and listen, yeah?"

"Don't forget, Etta, there is a fence around what is arguably the most famous gunslinger site in the state."

"But the fence is temporary, right?"

Molly crossed her arms over her chest and rolled her eyes.

"How about this?" Etta set Rosie on the floor and rose. "We'll go to the meeting and see what happens. We should head out, though. I need to drop Rosie off at my place."

"Yeah. That works." Molly grabbed her phone and followed Etta and Rosie out the door.

Between the dillydallying at Molly's place, Rosie's antics when they got to Etta's apartment, and the shot they decided to do at the bar before making their way over to town hall, they ended up being the last ones in the door before Mayor Wright called the meeting to order.

Molly and Etta slipped onto the bench at the very back of the hall, and Molly peered over the heads of what had to be nearly everyone who lived in town. Even the handful of kids who were residents sat between their parents with freshly combed hair.

"Holy shit," Etta said. "*Everyone* is here."

If this many people turned out, it must mean that they were every bit as leery about someone buying up Stan's property as she was. She scanned the audience and easily spotted Seph's impossibly shiny, flowing locks. She whispered to herself, "You're going down."

There was no way Seph could have heard her over the low murmuring of the townspeople, but she turned her head, and her gaze locked with Molly's. It lasted a fraction of a moment. But in that beat of time, an image flashed through Molly's brain. Seph, naked except for a pair of pink socks, lying across her bed, a wicked smile on her face.

Molly shook her head, breaking eye contact. She refocused on the long table at the front of the room. The mayor sat in the center, a gavel in her hand. She held it high and still as she said something to Margie Callahan, who sat on her left. On the other side of Margie was Kyle Jillian, the owner of the town restaurant and bar, and Etta's uncle. To the mayor's right sat Molly's father. Jeb Green held a lot of sway in Theia, and his place on the town council was practically guaranteed. Beside him was the newest council member, Mia Mulholland. Barely out of college, Mia was the youngest and most unpredictable of the bunch.

Molly knew all she needed was three votes. That was totally doable, a no-brainer. No one in their right mind would want to allow someone to purchase what rightfully belonged to the whole town.

Mayor Wright's gavel hit the table with a loud clap as she called the meeting to order. Molly sat patiently as they went through all the rigamarole of a council meeting. She'd been to several since she returned to town, and they were no more exciting than one would expect. In fact, until tonight, not more than a dozen people had ever attended, and that was the day they were debating the searingly hot issue of whether or not to pay to have the single traffic light in town replaced or put in a four-way stop.

Molly sighed. She hated that four-way stop.

But today would be different. Today, the whole town would turn on the enigmatic stranger with boatloads of cash, a stranger that only Molly knew had a perfectly round mole on her inner thigh.

"Now." Mayor Wright's voice boomed through the old building. "We have a presentation from Ms. Persephone Milan."

"It's Cosmo. Persephone Cosmo." Seph stood in front of the council.

Mayor Wright tipped her head. "So sorry, Ms. Cosmo."

"No trouble at all."

"Please proceed." The mayor gestured with one hand toward the podium set up at the head of the aisle.

There was no microphone on the podium, or anywhere in this small room that held only about sixty people, and as far as Molly knew the fifty-some jammed in here now was as close as they'd ever gotten to full capacity.

"Thank you so much. City council, Mayor, and people of Theia."

Molly leaned toward Etta. "Seriously, people of Theia. This woman is a cliché."

Etta's gaze stayed fixed on Seph. "*Shhhh.*"

"I'm delighted to be here as a new citizen of the town. As many of you may already know, in addition to the other buildings I will be speaking about, I also purchased the Bothwood home."

The old mansion sat next door to the Primrose, run-down and fading into history. It had been built by Theia's most successful gold miner in 1899. Just six years later the lode that supported so many individual claims would dry up, and the opulent mansion, along with the rest of the town, would be abandoned.

No one had wanted to commit the kind of cash it would take to restore the ten-room monstrosity to its former glory. Until now, apparently.

"I also bought the six cabins, the original general store,

the saddlery, the laundry, and the Warsaw saloon which Stan owned."

A wave of whispers and titters flowed through the room. Molly sat back silently. The tension was palpable, and she almost felt bad for Seph. This was going to be rough for her.

"My plan is a careful historic preservation project for the cabins, saddlery, and laundry that I own, along with as many of the cabins owned by other people that the owners will allow. I will carefully restore these buildings, to preserve them so visitors can go inside safely, see a little better what they may have originally looked like, free of charge. I will also restore the old hotel, based on a deal I just made this morning with its owner, and turn it into a museum dedicated to Theia's history. As for the saloon, that is the crown jewel of town. And I plan to renovate it and turn it into a working pub. Customers will be able to order a drink at the bar where Hugh Taft once stood, to play at the table where Bub Roy regularly ruled over a poker game, to waltz in through the swinging doors that Sheriff Tillman stepped through right before he shot and killed his cousin." Seph paused and looked around the room.

Her deep, rich brown eyes flittered past Molly, who was still caught up in an inexplicable desire to have them land on her, when Mayor Wright leaned forward.

"Ms. Milan. All of that sounds pretty great. But can you assure us that you're going to preserve the integrity of the historic nature of these buildings?"

Seph turned back to the mayor and flashed a sickeningly sweet smile. "Of course."

"To be clear, you plan to open the saloon as an operating bar?"

"Yes. But I'm going to do it while still carefully preserving the nature of the building."

A murmur ran through the room. Mayor Wright expressed the concern that was surely passing around the room on the wave of discontent that was palpable in the air. "The Warsaw is our most famous site. I think we're all a little concerned about what it means to turn it into a working business."

"There are a lot of historic buildings in this town that are operating either in the way they were originally or in a completely different way. This building for example, the Theia shop, the Primrose, the Oasis."

Mayor Wright nodded. "I do see your point. You intend the Warsaw to be like those?"

"I do. I think it deserves to be operating again. Visitors deserve to experience it the way people did over a century ago."

"Thank you for that explanation, Ms. Milan. Would you mind moving over here, and we'll open up the podium to anyone who has questions?"

Seph moved to stand near the long table, a gleaming smile planted on her face as if she were getting ready to present a new SUV at the Detroit Auto Show.

Molly could form at least a half dozen questions in her mind. Surely, with the whole town here, they could think of at least twice as many. But the room stayed eerily silent.

Molly was about to stand up and march to the wooden podium and was halfway out of her seat when Evelyn Cutter rose from her spot in the second row. Evelyn's opinion on this would be interesting. She was Stan's ex-wife. They'd split years ago but still acted like they were married. She was the owner and sole employee of the tourist shop, which was housed in what had been the original assay office. Now it sold cards, keychains, magnets, and T-shirts that said things like "I survived the showdown in Theia."

Everyone loved Evelyn. The respect for her was clear in the dead silence that awaited her words. She stepped up to the podium and cleared her throat. "I harassed Stan for a decade about those buildings." She shot her glare toward Stan, who perched on the bench in the front row. "I told him he needed to do something with all those buildings. He needed to quit messing around with the most important historic site in the great state of Montana and do something meaningful with it. And that's what we intended when we planned the historic park. Now it sounds to me that what you plan to do with most of the town is in line with that."

Seph nodded so hard she looked like a bobblehead.

"And I assume you're willing to let the historic preservation committee review those plans?" Evelyn raised one eyebrow and shot Seph a look that would have wilted a lesser person.

"Yes, ma'am. One hundred percent."

"I don't deny that I and others fixed up original buildings and turned them into shops and things. And I'm not saying I'd deny someone else the opportunity to do that. But the saloon is smack dab in the middle of the park we're trying to make. And if you're willing to help us make the park, as you say, how do we deal with that?"

Seph furrowed her brow. "I'm not sure I understand the problem."

Evelyn smiled. "I appreciate your honesty. We can talk about it over tea at my house tomorrow." And just like that, Evelyn turned on her heel and marched back to her seat.

An unceremonious grunt poured out of Molly's throat. Every eye in the place landed on her a second before Etta's arm dropped onto her shoulders. Someone coughed. Someone else giggled. Mayor Wright banged her gavel.

All eyes turned toward the mayor. "Would anyone else like to speak?" She practically speared Molly with her gaze.

Molly stood, tossed her hair off her forehead in an overdramatic head shake, and marched up the row toward the podium.

Molly glared at Seph. "What you don't understand, Ms. Milan, is that there are certain ways a ghost town park should look. Here in Montana, visitors to a ghost town expect certain things. And we all found out the hard way what happens when you ignore that. It's a town called Kekker. You should look it up."

Exactly as she'd planned, a wave of sound rose through the room, the collective sucking in of air at the mention of such a reviled place. Seph frowned, but she didn't speak, and she didn't look away.

"People don't want the old buildings to be broken up with new ones. They want to stay in that feeling that they are walking through a place completely abandoned to time."

Seph's chin rose. "Don't they also like to experience what it was like back then? I know that's why the Primrose is full every night during the season and why people love to eat at the Oasis. Their heads on a swivel the whole time they are in there, taking it all in, being in the place. The saloon will be like that."

"Yeah. But those places are outside the proposed park. You're talking about ruining the park concept itself with an open business right inside it."

Molly waited for a retort, but Seph stood there, staring at Molly.

Molly grinned. She'd won. Just like that. It was so much easier than she'd thought. She turned to go back to her seat, not willing to draw this out any longer.

"I would like to propose something."

Molly spun back around at the sound of Seph's voice.

Seph looked around the room, her gaze touching nearly every person. "I've already had conversations with the Greens." She flashed a simpering smile that had Molly's cheeks heating. "Who gave me wonderful new ideas. Now, if you'll give me some time to talk with Evelyn and others, I'll come up with a plan that will satisfy everyone. Then I'll hold a meeting, and we can all discuss this again."

Molly took a step toward Seph, passing the imaginary threshold the podium made. "Does that mean you'll stop construction and take down the fence?"

"No. I won't do that. However, I will talk to everyone and see what we can come up with."

Molly opened her mouth to protest, but Mayor Wright dropped her gavel. "That's it then. Meeting adjourned."

Chapter Five

The sounds echoing through Theia this early in the morning were nothing short of magical. The air was still, though the trees and bushes rustled with squirrels and chipmunks. Prairie dogs wove across the ground, their tiny claws scratching the rough surface while the threatening call of a Red-tailed hawk circling above disturbed their activities.

Molly took in a deep breath. Old wood, a hint of rot, morning dew, and the unmistakable scent of rich victory flowed through her. If there was one weapon she had, it was words, and she'd wielded them with precise accuracy. Okay. So maybe it was more than words. The post included a long diatribe from her about the dangers of private ownership of important historic sites, but it was the photo of Kekker beside one of Theia that was really going to push the historians, librarians, and those ever-present concerned citizens of Montana over the edge and join her campaign against Seph Milan.

She pushed her feet against the wood of the bed-and-breakfast's back porch. The old swing creaked as it swayed on its rockers. From here she could see the little house that had become her home. A few years before the Primrose was carefully built, in Theia's heyday, her cabin had been hastily thrown together to house Henry Moore while he tended to his mine and oversaw the building of the big house for his family.

It might have been intended to be a temporary dwelling, designed to be demolished after its grand neighbor was ready for its residents, but it was sturdy and, in its own way, beautiful. It had been saved from destruction when the completion of the big house coincided with the imminent arrival of Elizabeth Moore's eighth child. That resulted in her mother's insistence that she, as a widow with little to do aside from tend to her only daughter and grandkids, be available to help upon the arrival of the new child. Henry Moore, not being fond of his mother-in-law, had insisted that she have her own house.

So the cabin stayed on its quiet piece of land in the corner of the lot, and more than a hundred years later became Molly's home. When she came back from Seattle five years ago, Molly had planned to hide out in Theia for only a short time while she picked up the pieces of her life. But she'd found a path here, and once again the cabin that was originally intended to be temporary had become permanent.

"Nice day, huh?"

Molly's feet hit the porch so hard she felt the swing's frame quiver. She spun her head to find Seph standing a step beyond the back door, light playing in her rich, dark hair. Molly cleared her throat to cover her surprise. "Hi, Seph."

Seph glided across the porch, her light sandals seeming to float above the painted surface. "Molly." She lowered herself gracefully into the wicker chair beside Molly's swing, her gaze pointedly fixed on Molly's little house. "I heard you went to Seattle after graduation to work at a magazine."

"So we're doing this small talk thing then?"

"Yeah. We are. Seattle?"

Molly turned back to gaze at her home. She and her father had painted it themselves. The light blue complemented the Primrose's deep, sunshine yellow perfectly. She admired how clean it looked. It was her new beginning, her fresh start. Just the mention of the magazine dredged up the trauma the little cabin and her new life were trying to obliterate. And a wealthy woman, not unlike the one sitting across from her, with an irresistible body, a bag full of charm, and more money than she knew what to do with, had been at the heart of it all.

Molly had a practiced mask to keep her thoughts to herself, and she used it now. "Who'd you hear that from?"

"I don't know. Somebody from school. I don't remember."

"You were asking around about me?"

Seph rolled her eyes. "Are you going to answer the question?"

"I did go to Seattle. Then I came back here."

"So are you back for good?"

"I'm back for now."

"I see."

"What about you?" Molly turned to look at Seph. The intensely deep brown eyes she remembered way too well bored into her. "What are your post-divorce plans, minus the thing we're not talking about?"

Seph laughed. It was low and sweet, the sound reverberating through Molly's body like an earthquake. "I'm still figuring it out, to be honest. I worked hard to build a company that my husband took all the credit for. I'm ready for a vacation, and, frankly, I deserve it."

"Why did you let him take all the credit?"

"I didn't *let* him. I tried my damnedest to take the credit I deserved. But that's not how the world works, especially the tech world."

Something dark and rich bubbled up in Molly's chest, and she said something deeply unkind, despite the hit her conscience took. "So this is your solution then? You need something to put your name on, so you buy a famous historical site and slap your mark all over it. Seems like cheating to me."

The muscle at the edge of Seph's jaw flexed. Her fingers were folded together in her lap, knuckles white. "I wanted to do something meaningful with my money, something significant, but I guess you'll see it however you want to see it."

Molly stopped the swing by slamming her heels into the porch. "It didn't occur to you that maybe someone else was doing something significant here, too? You just glide into Theia," Molly threw her arms in the air, "I'm here, everyone! Ready to save you from your pointless existence with my ideas that I in no way ran by anyone already living and working here. Yay me!"

Seph bowed her head for a long beat. Then she looked back up. "Okay. So I didn't do my research before I bought. But I'm doing it now. I have a meeting with Evelyn today, and Stan and Mayor Wright as well. I'm trying to do better."

"People's livelihoods are here, Seph. And many of them don't have an extra month's pay to live off, let alone millions in the bank."

Seph huffed out a breath. "I'm not so far removed from my working-class upbringing that I'm oblivious to that. And I know that I'm affecting your business. I want to address that."

Molly wasn't sure which emotion was more prevalent, surprise or annoyance. "Don't worry about me."

Seph tilted her head. "I know that I've taken away a stop on the tour."

"The tours are about a third of my income these days. I can survive without them for a season."

"Oh!" Seph's brows rose to her hairline. "Yet you were so upset about the fence."

"I *am* upset by the fence. And it's not all about me. It's about the historic preservation of the town. While we're talking about my business, most of my income comes from book sales and speaking engagements. And I have those sales and those gigs because of the Warsaw. People who've been to town buy the book or book me as a speaker. People who've never been here look up photos and videos and news stories about the place online after they hear me talk or read my book. My audience is overcome by

Theia, enamored with it. But they are especially connected to the Warsaw, and taking it off the market temporarily sucks for my bottom line. But changing it completely, that's a disaster for me *and* the rest of the town."

"I don't think it has to be like that."

Molly pushed off with her feet again. The swing let out a loud squawk as it moved. "Again with the idea that you know better than the people who have been living here for over twenty years."

"That's not what I . . . I didn't . . ." Seph stood, her fists balled at her sides. "I think we should discuss this later."

"Fine. Whatever. Have fun being the queen of the town." Molly waved her fingers at Seph.

Seph marched back into the house, each step vibrating through the old wood.

Molly sat back in the swing. This was going to be one hell of a war.

Etta poured the glass of wine with extreme precision. From her perch at the bar Molly tracked her movements. "My mom was right, I should have started something up with you before we ended up in the friend zone. We could be married right now."

Etta slid the glass across the wood top. "You couldn't handle me." Her gaze flickered up. "He's here."

Molly spun on the barstool as Kyle Jillian slipped in the back door. He waved at Molly and Etta as his long legs carried him across the small space. Kyle had been a basketball player in his college days, and he still held that physique. Etta claimed that her uncle's secret was that he worked out constantly. His home, which sat on the very edge of town, stood out not only because it was new rather than renovated, but also because it was the only one that featured a gym. He was beloved in town anyway, but the fact that he opened his gym up to anyone who wanted to use it only endeared him further.

Kyle slid onto the barstool beside Molly and accepted the drink Etta had prepared for him. Molly examined the glass filled with a yellowish-green liquid, but she could not decipher what on earth it was.

He lifted his glass. "Nice to see you, Molly."

"You too. Thanks for meeting with me."

He took a long drink and set his glass down with a thump. "Sure. Etta said it was urgent."

"It is. It's about Seph buying the town and doing this whole renovation project."

He tapped his finger on his chin. "I listened last night. I thought her ideas about preserving the old buildings was in line with what the rest of us have been planning and, I must say, generous since she's planning to foot the bill."

"It doesn't concern you to have one person—an outsider who has showed up on the scene out of nowhere—have control over the town like that?"

Kyle stroked his chin and looked up at the ceiling. "I don't know about control. She's on board with getting historic designation, so that would really limit what she can do."

Molly dropped her hand on the bar, fingers spread. She distinctly remembered Seph tapping her finger over the paperwork and pointing out that her signature was not there. And she hadn't said a thing about historic designation at the town council meeting. "How do you know that?"

"She told me. She said she would file an amendment giving her consent as the new owner so it wouldn't hold up the process."

"When did she tell you this?"

"This morning. We had breakfast at the Primrose and talked about some things."

"What things?"

Etta leaned on the bar, inserting herself into the small circle. "Yeah. What things?"

Kyle flashed a half smile and took a leisurely sip of his drink. "She wants to buy one of the buildings I own, and I'm not discussing the details with the two of you." He gestured to them both with the glass still in his hand. "But, as a result of her offer, I dug deeper and asked a lot of questions about her plans."

"Like what?" Etta asked.

"You know, same things that came up at the meeting. What are her ultimate goals? How is she going to collaborate with everyone else? Why Theia?"

That last question snagged Molly like a tree branch on a narrow trail. "What did she say about that? The why Theia thing?"

Kyle shrugged. "Her reasons were as good as anyone else's."

"Yeah." Etta dropped her hand on Kyle's wrist. "So what were they?"

Kyle shook his head. "Not my place to say. You'll have to ask her."

Molly twirled the stem of her wine glass between her thumb and forefinger. She decided to change the subject before she lost Kyle altogether. "What about the saloon? She wants to open it as an actual bar. Even if she can do that and preserve historic designation, she's creating competition for you."

"If she can get all the permits, yeah. There are a few steps first. She doesn't even have a liquor license yet."

Etta leaned her elbows on the bar. "I doubt that will be an issue. I don't remember the last time someone didn't get a liquor license."

Kyle shrugged and took another sip. "This is really good, Etta. Damn."

"I'm an excellent bartender."

Molly slapped her hand on the bar. "Exactly! See! This is a big problem."

Uncle and niece turned to look at her with identical expressions of confusion on their faces. It was Etta who asked, "What's the connection here?"

"She's going to put you out of business!"

"The restaurant?" Kyle shook his head. "No way. Even if she did sell food, which she's not planning to do and I don't know where the hell you'd put a kitchen in that place, we're packed all summer. I'm not worried about it. I told Evelyn to open up a deli in the back of the store if she wants to. I'm not threatened."

"What about the bar?" Why was no one in this town connecting the dots? Molly felt like some sort of overzealous Captain Obvious.

"Oh, sure. Probably." Kyle shrugged.

"That doesn't bother you?"

"No. I mean, the bar without the restaurant would be a money loser. I only keep it as an entity separate from the restaurant as a gift to the locals."

Molly wanted to scream. Instead she turned to Etta. "You'll be out of a job."

"No, I won't. I spend most of my time filling restaurant drink orders."

Molly dropped her head on the bar in an attempt to control the wave of frustration moving through her. Etta's hand touched the top of her head. "Maybe this won't be so bad."

Molly lifted her head and peered at them both. "What if this whole thing goes the way of Kekker? She owns almost half the town, probably more soon since she's apparently snapping up every building she can find. She could literally wreck us all."

Etta bit her lip, and Molly knew this worried her. Kyle laughed. "Don't pull the Kekker card, Molly. That was one idiotic dude who did a really stupid thing. And no one was around to stop him. He owned the whole town, and no one lived there. This is not at all the same thing. If Persephone throws up a neon sign and bricks over old wood, we're all here to see it and do something about it."

"What if we can't stop her? She has more money than all of us combined. She might sound nice and reasonable and generous now. But people can change, just like that." She snapped her fingers in the air, and as she did a memory flashed in her mind of Kelsy, her cold eyes piercing Molly to her very soul.

Kyle chuckled. "What are you really upset about, Molly? Because every time someone tries to assuage your fears you keep pushing back."

There was no way she could articulate the links in her mind between past and present even if she wanted to open that drawer and yank all the contents out for everyone to see. So she focused on her core argument. "I've spent the last five years writing about and giving tours of the ghost town. Like everyone else, I've made my living on the history of this place. I don't want someone to mess that up. And, honestly, I can't understand why I'm alone in this. Everyone living in Theia owes their living to the ghost town. *Every one of us*. And yet you all are willing to let some stranger from California put all that in jeopardy because she needs a project to distract her after a divorce in which she made millions of dollars. I don't get it."

Kyle rubbed his chin between his thumb and forefinger. "It sounds to me like you have a problem with the woman herself rather than her plans."

Molly took a slow sip of her wine, her gaze focused on the clear rim of the glass. She refused to let her feelings about Seph be a part of what was behind her battle to keep Theia as it should be. This fight was for the good of the whole town. Hell, it was what was best for the entire state of Montana. "This is about preserving our history, our economy, and our dignity."

Kyle grinned. "Sure it is." He turned to Etta. "What's the story there?"

"No idea."

"Hmmm." Kyle stroked his chin. "I smell some history."

Etta eyed Molly. Best friend or not, she didn't know about Seph and Molly's past. But the way Molly was squirming under their scrutiny was about to give her away. She tried to cover.

"This isn't about Seph, it's about Theia. Can we please focus?"

Kyle slapped a hand on her shoulder. "Sorry, Molly. I'm willing to explore Persephone's ideas. And I certainly welcome the presence of someone like her in our town. Why don't you bury the hatchet on whatever issues you have with her and focus on what Theia needs and how we can steer Persephone toward that. No need being stressed out about the things you can't change."

Those words "something you can't change" jammed into her chest with the same force they had the day she'd left Seattle, powerless and hopeless. Still, Molly blatantly ignored it all. "No way." She stood up, causing her barstool to wobble and Rosie to shoot her a look of reproach. "I'm not going to let this stand. Even if I have to carry this torch alone until the rest of the town comes to its senses."

As she marched out of the bar she heard Kyle's amused voice call out to her, "Good luck with that, Molly."

Chapter Six

Molly sifted through the bankers box methodically, pulling out every folder and leafing through the contents as if each one was a treasure chest. Since she wasn't entirely certain what she was looking for, the whole exercise felt a bit aimless. Each folder held a new memory from her time at Berkeley.

She'd saved the strangest things: a certificate stating that she'd earned her junior ranger badge at Point Reyes National Seashore; her old student ID with the picture so washed out it was impossible to tell if she was a human or an apparition; paper coasters from a variety of Bay Area bars; and theater tickets.

She had carefully cataloged each piece and the associated memory and was nearly at the end of the box's precious contents when she found it. No doubt her subconscious had this object in mind when she'd randomly decided to sort through mementos.

She pulled the object out of a stiff envelope. It being the sole occupant betrayed its importance, no matter how much Molly might like to ignore that now. To fit it in the folder, Molly had folded it in half. Long and thin, designed to be stapled to a light pole, the poster announced a pre-graduation party that promised to be Berkeley's biggest bash.

For beer money and food to donate to the local foodbank, everyone who was about to graduate was welcome. Molly actually had taken the poster down two days after the party. She'd told herself, and the friend that was with her, that it was to help the organizers with post-party cleanup. She'd kept that poster, not because she didn't want to add to the piles of recyclable paper that sat about campus at the end of the year like monuments to late-night writing binges, but because she wanted to remember that party.

The fresh breeze that had kept the warm air from being stifling had not affected the inside of the house, which, stuffed with bodies, approached oven status. Molly had followed Glenn and Troy through a maze of people, most of whom had stood in small groups, elbows bent as they held or sipped on drinks.

The house was older than the one that housed Molly's apartment, and the closed-off rooms mirrored a lot of other early to mid-twentieth-century houses in Berkeley. While she hadn't been to a party at this exact location before, she could practically make the turns with her eyes closed as they made their way to the back of the house. Their trio had to pause at the door to the kitchen. A superhighway of people went in to get or refill drinks while others ducked out with full cups balanced in both hands.

"Troy, get us something. We're gonna go see who's here." Troy nodded as Glenn turned and touched Molly's elbow lightly. She took the hint and moved them away from the fast-paced line. Glancing around, she caught sight of a fluffy sectional couch that was half empty and headed that way.

Glenn's goal at any party was always to determine who was there, first and foremost. That way he could properly assess who he wanted to mingle with and who he wanted to avoid. Troy preferred to sit in a small group and talk only to his friends. Molly was fully in between. So she made it her goal to find a place where Troy could relax, and she and Glenn could scan the crowd.

The couch promised to be the sweet spot at this gathering, and they dropped gratefully into it, leaving enough space for Troy's skinny ass.

"I feel like I should know more people here than I do," Glenn said.

Molly had nodded. This party was only for people about to graduate. So in theory, that limitation should have bred at least some level of familiarity. But Berkeley was a big school, and literally every graduate had gotten the notice. So finding themselves in a sea of strangers should not have been a surprise. "Pretty sure I saw that guy you dated freshman year. The one with the terrible mustache."

"Oh my god. Saw him. Avoided him. Can you believe he still has that same mustache? I know people told him it was a bad one because I did. And I like mustaches. Think they're sexy, but his—oh wait. He's right there." Glenn turned his head into Molly's shoulder as she chuckled.

Mustache guy moved away without stopping to talk. Molly scanned the crowd for Troy. He was emerging from the kitchen as another person was passing him to enter. The long waves of rich, dark hair caught Molly's attention. She knew that hair.

Seph Cosmo flashed the deepest, sexiest set of eyes Molly had ever seen her way for a fraction of a moment, and it had Molly nearly melting right there on a stranger's couch. Then Seph turned to disappear into the kitchen.

Molly tried to pull her shit together as Troy approached with three plastic cups balanced in his hands, a grimace on his face. She and Glenn helped him unload his loot, and they all settled back on the couch.

While Glenn and Troy discussed the people they might know, including the close call with mustache dude, Molly watched the kitchen doorway. In there somewhere was Seph Cosmo. And with any luck, she'd come out and give Molly another look at that swirly sundress she was wearing.

Ten minutes later, Molly was about to give up, resigned to the idea that Seph must have gotten pulled into one of those kitchen conversations where everyone plants themselves against the counter and stays there.

And then she showed up again.

Her head was turned away at first as she said something to a person out of sight. Then she swung around to face Molly's direction, her hair flying around her shoulders. She held two clear plastic wine glasses, each at least two-thirds full of a bright red.

Molly might have stopped to wonder who the other glass was for. But her mind never got the chance to wander away from Seph's form moving toward her, eyes holding Molly's gaze the entire time.

She floated across the space until she stood directly in front of Molly. "Molly, right?" Seph tipped her head.

Molly's mouth was so dry she had to peel it open to speak. "Yeah. We've had a couple classes together."

"We did. I'm Seph."

Molly stopped herself from saying, "I know." They'd never had a real conversation, and the massive crush she'd harbored on Seph from afar was certainly not something she needed to expose. Instead, she managed to nod and smile.

"Would you like a drink?" Seph held out one of the wine glasses.

Molly shoved the half-empty plastic cup of whatever weird punch Troy had fetched her toward Glenn. He took it and made a sound that let Molly know, without glancing his way, that he was completely aware of what was happening in front of him.

The grunt was followed by, "Why don't you ladies go out on the porch where it's quieter and you can talk?"

As soon as Molly took the wine glass from her hand, Seph glanced around. Her gaze landed on a spot behind Molly for a moment before she looked back. "I would like that. Would you?"

Molly shot up. "Yeah. Cool."

Seph moved through the crowd with Molly at her heels. She found a sliding glass door, pulled it open, and plunged out onto a rotting wooden deck. Molly shut the door behind her, muting the sounds of the party and enveloping Seph and her in the dark night air.

Seph leaned on the railing, setting her drink on the peeling paint and staring out at the city. Molly followed suit. The porch sat in the bottom of a small yard, the multistory buildings on all sides hemming it in, creating a private, intimate place in the middle of the city. Molly loved it—overgrown weeds, neglected fruit trees, and all.

"I've been hoping to talk to you."

Molly turned toward Seph. With her eyes adjusting to the dark, she could see Seph's outline clearer. Her beauty threatened to stop Molly's lungs from working. But she managed to speak. And what came out was the deepest truth. "I've been wanting to talk to you for two years."

"I wish you would have."

Molly was about to say the same to Seph, but something told her not to. Seph carried a sadness Molly couldn't quite grasp, and she didn't want to throw anything at her that felt like blame. "I have to admit," Molly turned toward Seph, "I didn't talk to you because I would have been inclined to flirt with you."

Seph turned as well, their torsos perfectly lined up a few feet away from one another. "I like the sound of that."

"Yeah?"

"Yeah."

"But, um. I kind of thought you had a boyfriend."

"I did. Which," Seph sighed, "means that I spent most of my college life not getting hit on by the likes of you."

"And that makes you sad."

"Very sad."

Molly moved closer to Seph. "And the boyfriend? Where is he now?"

Seph let out a harumph. "Not here."

"Not here."

"And not my boyfriend anymore." Seph moved her hand toward Molly. She stopped, her fingers hovering in the open air. Then they closed the space and landed on Molly's wrist. "But you're here."

"I am most certainly here."

The images from that night clicked through Molly's mind like an old school slideshow. They'd spent hours on that porch. Moonlight had peered through sparse clouds and lit the space enough for Molly to make out Seph's perfect curves, the way her hands moved as she spoke, and the depth in her brown eyes.

When and how they had decided to walk back to Molly's apartment wasn't something she'd kept in the memory vault, but she did recall the slow stroll through the streets of Berkeley. Even clearer was the feeling in her gut when she'd shut the door of her apartment with Seph on the inside.

She closed her eyes as she remembered that first kiss. Her throat let out a little moan as she recalled the way Seph's skin felt against hers and how it tasted. The way her mouth pulled the rich sounds of pleasure from Seph.

Molly opened her eyes and dropped the poster. This was a terrible idea. That one night and what came after had no bearing on the present. The past had no relevance in the here and now. She picked up the poster and shoved it to the bottom of the box before slamming on the lid.

She would forget that Seph was anything more than her adversary in the battle for Theia.

Chapter Seven

Molly glared at the fence. Even though it was still the object of her ire, it was no longer the main thing blocking her guests' view of the famous pub. Now, scaffolding ringed the entire building, beneath which workers came and went from the gaping opening that had once held crooked saloon doors and now was a terrible, empty hole.

The Warsaw wasn't the last stop on her tour anymore. She'd adjusted the route to make the old hotel the last stop. She used the ghost story about the woman in white who'd been seen in the upstairs window on several dark, spooky nights as her new closing tale. It was okay as far as stories went, but nothing compared to the saloon's showdown.

The biggest problem with her tour was that this infernal eyesore took away from the overall ambience of the town. It pulled her guests out of the mood she tried so hard to set. It was so bad that she'd tried to plot out a tour through town that avoided the saloon altogether, but the route had been pretty ridiculous with a ton of backtracking and looping around. She'd done it for three days, but in the end her guests asked about the saloon anyway. Of course they did. They booked Molly's tours precisely because they'd either read her book or seen her speak.

Which meant that this was really all her own fault. She'd made the saloon famous and created a legendary space that had become a must-see among ghost town relics in the state.

She'd written that first book about Theia while nursing a broken heart and bruised ego in the little cabin on her parents' property. In the midst of her deep depression over losing her job and her girlfriend all in one fantastically epic life failure, her father had forced her out of the house to help with a project to clear out the files in Theia's old courthouse.

The goal was to sort through them to determine what should be donated to the state archives and what should be kept in the local library housed in one corner of the regal building. She'd gone, very much against her will. Sorting and moping were the themes of the several days she spent combing through every file that had survived over a hundred and twenty years in a dusty basement.

Somewhere along the way, she'd started to pay attention. Those dirty old boxes contained rich stories, woven through complex primary documents. The puzzle begged to be put together. She grabbed onto the challenge with a fervor that pulled her out of the molasses of her pain.

She'd written her first Theia book all about Bub Roy and his demise at the hands of his cousin, Sheriff Tillman, during a spectacular showdown at the Warsaw Saloon. The second and third books delved into other stories of the town, including the vigilante committee that had formed following Bub's death. That group of supposed do-gooders had rounded up alleged outlaws in a controversial fashion. She also wrote about the Cole family, who at one point ran the entire town before a delicious scandal had them all fleeing in the middle of the night.

That first book was her bread and butter. Because of it, she now made her living as a writer, and her tours of the town were sold out for months in advance. Not even Shannon McGregor could put a dent in her popularity.

But this fence could.

"What are they doing to it?" Kelly Wright was the organizer of this tour group. She was the development director for the museum in Bozeman, and she brought donors on Molly's tour once a year. She was loud and funny, and Molly thoroughly enjoyed her.

"Desecrating it."

Kelly turned with a look of disgust comically painted on her face. "Seriously? How is this legal?"

"The person who bought it wants to restore it and turn it into a working bar." Molly could hear the defeat in her own voice.

"Sounds like Kekker all over again. Can't anyone stop this?"

Molly shook her head. "I've tried."

"Hey there!"

Molly swiveled to see Seph standing inside the fence and waving her hands above her head.

Most of the two dozen museum donors waved back.

Seph marched toward them. "Would you all like to come inside?"

Before Molly could even figure out what the hell was happening, the group was shouting its consent.

"Come this way." Seph waved them along the fence line until they reached a gate. She swung it open and threw her arm out as if she were a magician presenting her greatest trick.

Molly followed at the very back as the group stepped into Seph's lair.

"I'm Seph Cosmo. It's nice to meet you all. I'm sorry about the construction, but we're restoring the Warsaw to its former glory."

The crowd tittered and threw out words of thanks. The way they stared at Seph, as if she were a celebrity gracing them with her presence, twisted a knife in Molly's gut. But she was stuck. When Kelly and a few others turned to her for guidance, she plastered on her best guide's smile as if this were all part of her plan.

"I've asked the crew to take a break," Seph said. "So you can go in with your guide and get the entire experience." She once again gestured with her long arm, perfectly manicured nails waving toward the saloon's entrance.

Molly tried her best to sound chipper. "Okay, go on in, and once we're all in there we'll gather by the bar." Assuming it's still there.

The group moved toward the entrance and Molly followed slowly, her gaze hitting Seph as she passed. Was she supposed to thank her? Was she supposed to grovel because Seph had given her back what had been there for the taking before she so greedily stole it?

Seph got nothing more than Molly's cold shoulder, but if she was surprised, she didn't show it. She simply spun on a pair of sturdy boots and headed toward the back of the saloon where workers gathered around a cloth-covered table.

Molly wasn't sure what she expected to see when she walked into the Warsaw. Perhaps some of the floorboards ripped up, or some of the walls partially torn into. Maybe fresh boards where there had once been gaps. At the very least she expected that the newspaper covering the far wall—its yellow, tattered pages clinging to rough boards, peeling away in some places—would be gone.

Instead, she saw some equipment, new wiring, some portable lights, and tools scattered about the space. But otherwise, it was exactly the same. Not only was the bar still there, right where it had always been, but dust motes on its surface appeared to be wholly undisturbed.

She positioned herself in the usual spot, behind the bar looking out at her group as if they were patrons and she their bartender. "Hugh Taft stood in this spot fourteen hours a day on every day but Sunday from April 5, 1886, when he opened the saloon to October 1, 1905, when he closed it forever. The saloon's life, like that of the town itself, was punctuated with a lot of excitement. When the lode's profits hit a hundred thousand dollars—that's over three million dollars in today's money—the miners celebrated right here. The first time a stagecoach was robbed on the road leading from here to Butte, Beck Gibbons came in here to tell everyone the news and round up a posse to hunt for the robbers. Not long after, Sheriff Tillman was pinned with his badge right down the road at the courthouse and walked over here minutes later to buy everyone in the bar a round."

Molly leaned over, her elbows resting on the bar. Her audience was captivated now, no longer looking around at the solid oak beams or the remnants of spindle back chairs stacked in the corner, but focused solely on her. "And you know who was in this bar the day his cousin was made sheriff, don't you?"

They all nodded.

"Bub Roy always sat right over there." She pointed to a corner with a table she knew wasn't the right one, but one that Stan had placed there years ago as a stand-in. "He was the king of the poker table. People used to say that he was here nearly as much as Hugh. Bub was considered to be an honest dealer, a friendly competitor, and an all-around nice guy. He was nearly as beloved as his lawman kin. But . . ."

The audience was barely breathing now, stuck on Molly's every word. This was the best part of her job. "He would disappear for weeks, sometimes months, at a time. And no matter how much prying every busybody in town did, including the local madam, Gretta Green—" she paused as eyes widened, and she grinned. "Yes, related. My great-great-great-grand aunt as a matter of fact. Anyway, even Gretta, who's said to have had a special relationship with Bub, if you know what I mean—" she winked, and her audience laughed.

"Even she couldn't get him to say where he went or what he was doing. But Sheriff Tillman caught wind of it one terrible day in August 1899. He got a letter from the governor saying that Bub was the most wanted man in the state. The governor claimed that his mother's sister's son, Bub Roy, was in fact the legendary robber and gunslinger, Blue Boots. Now I know what you're thinking, the name Blue Boots doesn't exactly strike terror in your hearts. But let me tell you, it did to the good people of Montana back then. Blue Boots was an outlaw known for robbing stagecoaches. But he did more than take the money of rich passengers. He killed any man who tried to resist him. He was called Blue Boots because he had the stain of the blue bloods he killed on his boots."

The silence in the room was disturbed by subtle gasps. Molly plunged back into her story. "One of the women who watched her husband die at the hands of Blue Boots was Lily McKittrick. Her husband owned the most successful mining operation in the state, over in Butte. She made it her mission to find out who Blue Boots really was and bring him to justice. So she traveled across the state and met with every madam and lady of the night she could find. She carried with her a drawing of Blue Boots' face."

Molly stood up straight and brandished both hands, fingers splayed. "No less than ten different women identified Bub Roy as Blue Boots. So Lily went to the governor with this information. And he put out a bounty on Bub. So on that fateful day, August 22, right here in this very saloon," Molly jammed her finger into the wooden bar, "Bub was conducting a poker game right over there." She pointed to the chair Stan had found in the courthouse basement and placed behind the stand-in poker table. Her audience's heads swiveled to follow her gesture. "Hugh was here, serving up drinks. And Sheriff Tillman walked in that door." She shifted their attention again, this time to the empty opening to her left. "With the wanted poster, the one that featured Lily McKittrick's drawing of Bub, clutched in his hand."

Molly made a fist with her right hand as if she herself were grasping the paper. "He walked in and announced to his first cousin that he was under arrest. Bub stood up slowly, like he didn't have a care in the world. He put his hand on his hip. Some people say he was going for his gun. Others say his hand was nowhere near it. But either way, his words were clear, even if his intentions were not. He said, 'I'm not gonna be arrested.' And that's when the sheriff shot."

A gasp echoed through the old wooden building.

"Some people claim that Bub was planning to pull his gun and shoot. They say the sheriff was justified. Others say that not only was Bub not going to shoot, but that he was actually innocent of the crimes he was accused of. Those voices were loud enough that Sheriff Tillman was run out of town. He went to Butte where he served as Lily McKittrick's personal bodyguard until he died of consumption on October 31, 1905, ironically the exact same day that Theia was abandoned by its very last resident and became a ghost town."

Molly shifted her weight so that she leaned back on her heels. "And that, my friends, is the story of the great showdown at the Warsaw."

Despite the noise of twenty-five people clapping, Molly detected a sound from behind her. She turned to see Seph Cosmo standing in the door to the back hallway. She leaned against the wall as if she'd been there for some time, clapping and grinning like the Cheshire Cat.

Chapter Eight

Molly knew the right thing to do. She'd been taught to be a kind, gracious person since childhood. She could not, despite her feelings of angst at her parents for harboring Seph and refusing to support her battle against Seph's plans, disappoint them by being an asshole.

So she stood in the hallway on the third floor of the Primrose with her hand hovering in front of Seph's door. She sighed, gave in, and knocked. This was happening whether she liked it or not.

It was only a matter of seconds before the door swung open, revealing Seph in tight leggings and an ivory blouse that swam around her curves like waves around a scenic rock on the ocean shore. Seph tipped her head. Her dark hair was draped over her shoulders elegantly. It was five thirty on a Thursday, and she looked like she was ready for a photo shoot.

Molly let out a hard breath. "Hi."

Seph stood back and waved her arm, the way she had for Molly's tour guests a couple of hours ago. Molly stepped into the room and immediately made her way to the high-backed chair that sat against the far wall. Her goal was to be gracious and friendly, not an easy task in this situation. So she figured taking a seat would be a good start.

Seph moved smoothly across the room toward an antique

table under the window. "Your mom installed this amazing espresso machine in here. Would you like something?"

"Yes, please."

"Would you like a latte or a cappuccino?"

"Just a straight espresso is good, thanks."

Seph set two of the delicate ivory mugs beneath the double spout. "Straight black espresso. I can see that."

Molly wasn't about to scoff. She also believed that how a person took their coffee was a reflection of their personality. "What about you?"

Seph hit grind and paused as the blades hitting beans created a brief cacophony. When it was done, she shrugged before pouring the ground espresso into the machine. "I'm very flexible. I basically like it all ways."

Molly had literally never met a person who didn't have at least some preference in how they took their coffee. She was still wrapping her head around that when Seph pulled the mugs out from under the twin spouts and presented one to Molly. After Molly took it, Seph perched on the edge of the bed with her own cup nestled in her hands.

Seph seemed to be waiting for Molly to speak, which made perfect sense. But as Molly sat there, the warmth from the mug seeping through the skin of her palms, she found herself incapable of speaking.

Seph must have grown tired of Molly's silence. "I liked your story. Very much."

"Thank you." Now that Seph had brought up the reason for this visit, it activated Molly's tongue. "I came to thank you for letting us in today. The tour, I mean. Thank you for letting my tour in so I could, you know, tell the story."

"You tell it way better than Shannon McGregor."

Molly was pretty sure she made a face at the mention of Shannon's name. But if she did, Seph didn't see it. She was gazing out the window.

"Thanks. I mean, it's not a competition." That was a complete lie. After her book had ended up on a few history shows and then hit a few big lists, Molly had placed an announcement on social media that she'd train a tour guide who wanted to take over her main business so she could focus on writing and speaking and give a handful of specialty tours. Instead of getting a budding entrepreneur full of heart, Shannon McGregor, an independently wealthy, bored empty-nester with a real estate broker husband, started her own specialty tours out of Bozeman, stealing everything she could from Molly's books, talks, and online blogs about Theia. So, yeah, it was a whole thing.

But that wasn't important right now. "How does she feel about you buying the saloon?"

Seph moved her gaze back to Molly. "Shannon? Oh, it was her idea. I mean, sort of." Her eyebrows knitted. "To be honest, exactly how it all went down is still a little unclear."

Molly tilted her head. "What do you mean?"

Seph shrugged. "I don't know. I was in a bad place. I went on this tour with Shannon, and now I own the saloon."

Molly leaned so far forward the hem of her shirt dipped into her drink. "Are you saying it was a mistake?"

Seph's eyes narrowed. "I didn't say that." She settled back in her chair and took a slow sip of coffee. "I'm not going to apologize for the trajectory I'm on."

"But it sounds to me like you don't even know what that trajectory is."

Seph stood quickly. "Here's the thing." She dropped her mug on the dresser with a crisp thud. "Your family's history in this place doesn't make you some sort of gatekeeper. You don't have more rights to it than me. If you really want to get into it, this land belongs to the Nez Perce."

Molly mirrored Seph's actions, even if her placing the mug on the table was not nearly as dramatic, and having to look up about three inches to stare Seph in the eyes didn't give her quite as much power as she'd like. "I never said I had some sort of claim on this place."

Seph sighed. "I'm sorry. I was thinking. I realize I robbed you of a great spot to tell your story. And while I wish I could stop construction for all of your tours, that simply isn't possible. But we could film your speech in the Warsaw, and you could show it to your guests."

"So I'm supposed to hold up a phone and show them a video of the place?"

"Well, I was thinking like a projector set up in the sitting room of the Primrose or something."

"What's the point of coming here to watch a video? Might as well stay home and see a documentary."

Seph took a step closer. In the tight space, they were practically pressed together, the toes of Seph's designer sandals nearly kissing the rubber tops of Molly's clogs. "Why are you so stubborn?" Seph cocked her head. The warm highlights in her thick curls peeked out at Molly as her hair dropped over her shoulder.

Molly ripped her mind away from imagining what that hair would feel like flowing through her fingers and met Seph's gaze. "Because you waltzed into *my* town, bought half of it, and then used your experience with whatever San Francisco publicist you've been working with for the past few years to spin this so I'm somehow the villain in this story."

Seph leaned forward. "I'm sorry, what were you saying about not being possessive? And I'm not the one doing the publicity stunt. You've already created an entire story around this." She waved her hands in a wide circle. One manicured finger nearly hit Molly's chin on its way around. "You have crafted a tale where *I'm* some sort of evil mastermind who found my way to this tiny town in the middle of absolutely nowhere just to fuck with you. When, in reality, I didn't know you were here. I thought you were in Seattle. And I came here to hide out from my own fucked-up life, not to mess up yours."

As soon as she finished her speech, Seph stepped back, her face draining as if all the heat had left her in that moment. Molly moved forward, keeping the distance between them exactly the same as it had been. "Is that why you're here? To hide?"

Seph shook her head. Her eyes roamed around the room before landing back on Molly's face. "I've been telling people that I have an ancestor that was here. And it turns out that I have a distant cousin who was here for about six months, but he was working a part of the lode that didn't produce and left. That's not my why. The truth is, I was deeply lonely, and something about Theia touched me when I needed it most."

Nothing in the world was more relatable to Molly. She lifted one hand slowly. Seph didn't move away, so Molly gently gripped Seph's upper arm. "I think maybe we got off on the wrong foot."

Seph's laugh was soft. "You think?"

This close to Seph, Molly was surrounded by her scent, breezy and fresh, like expensive laundry hung out to dry on the most spectacular summer day. Warmth flowed from Seph's arm through Molly's palm and traveled up through her to strike her in the chest. Seph leaned forward, almost an infinitesimal amount, but it brought her face closer to Molly's. Everything in the room had shifted, and what was coming was as obvious and inevitable now as the end had been for Theia on the day the mines stopped producing.

Molly waited for Seph to stop this madness. She had done nothing but fight Seph from the moment she arrived in town. Surely the last thing Seph would want was to close that space between them.

Molly lifted her right foot off the ground and slowly brought it back. Once that foot was back on the ground, her body would follow, taking her away from Seph, giving them both room to breathe. At that point, sanity had to return. Before that could happen, Seph reached up one hand and placed her palm on the back of Molly's head. Her fingers were woven into Molly's short locks, and she pulled.

Their lips slammed together, crashing into each other with a near violent force. While Molly had anticipated the kiss, she had not foreseen this. There was nothing slow and tentative about this kiss. It wasn't sweet and subtle like their very first kiss had been all those years ago.

Molly wrapped her arms around Seph's waist and tugged, pressing their bodies together. She answered Seph's insistent licking at the seam of her lips and opened her mouth. Seph was not only taller than Molly, but also stronger. Molly had felt Seph's firm bicep muscle earlier. Now she felt that power as Seph wrapped an arm behind her back and steered them both toward the wall beside the dresser. Seph's other hand reached out and cushioned Molly's fall backward.

Caught between the textured wallpaper and Seph's body was not at all a bad place to be. Molly ran her hands around Seph's waist then plunged them under Seph's blouse and trailed them across her ribcage. Seph's fingers, still tangled in Molly's hair, tightened on her locks as Molly's slipped over the lacy cups of Seph's bra. Seph's other hand deftly unzipped Molly's jeans and swiftly shimmied them down to her knees.

Molly pulled her mouth away, and Seph instantly began to suckle at her neck. With her lips beside Seph's ear, Molly whispered. "Let me taste you."

Seph released Molly's skin from between her teeth and let out a moan.

"I'm gonna take that as a yes." Molly spun them around so that Seph was against the wall. She kicked her jeans off, which gave her much greater freedom of movement, and she used it to drop to her knees.

Back at Berkeley on that one steamy night, Seph had been wearing a cute, flouncy dress. But today she'd been at a construction site and wore a pair of practical leggings. They posed only a slightly bigger challenge. Molly managed to get them out of her way so she could focus on slowly divesting Seph of the lacy panties that Molly imagined perfectly matched the bra she'd only felt with the tips of her fingers.

Molly looked up at Seph. She leaned against the wall as if she were melting into it, her head dropped down so she could look at Molly there on her knees. Dark curls, like hanging gardens, created a curtain around her face. But Molly could see the intensity in her eyes. Seph wanted this as much as Molly did.

Molly flashed Seph a smirk before she pressed her thumbs to the inside of her thighs, spreading Seph's legs farther apart, and then dipped forward and tasted. With the first flick of her tongue, Seph cried out. Somewhere in the back of Molly's mind she knew she should care about how easily sound carried through this old house, but it was far too irrelevant in this moment. Instead, her singular care was to keep that sound coming.

Her own moans were completely obliterated by Seph's. Each little nuance, each change of direction or speed from Molly elicited a matching response from Seph. It was intoxicating. Molly pulled back three times in an effort to prolong the pleasure. Seph didn't complain. Instead, she took deep, heaving breaths, bracing herself for the next onslaught.

Molly didn't stop when Seph's keening grew louder and her legs began to shake. Molly held her up, pressing her hips into the wall as she took Seph to the brink and pushed her right over the edge.

How they ended up on the bed moments later wasn't entirely clear. But there they were, Seph naked from the waist down, Molly in her underwear, lying the wrong way across the bed. Seph caged Molly's head with her arms and hovered her lips above hers. "Are you still?"

"Yes. I only top." Molly ran her hand over Seph's smooth bottom. "But, just like back then, I like being naked and doing things like this." Seph pressed her thigh between Molly's, and

Molly gave her a searing kiss in reward. "Does that bother you?"

Seph shook her head. "Not then and not now."

"I suppose you probably haven't been with a lot of women in between. You got engaged at graduation. The day after we . . . you know."

"Yeah. I'm a bit rusty."

Molly kissed Seph again. "No, you're not."

Seph laughed and pulled herself up so she was straddling Molly. "You think the whole bed-and-breakfast heard us?"

"You *are* pretty loud, but I don't care." Molly sat up so that Seph was in her lap and she could reach her lips for a kiss. "Fuck 'em. The sound of you coming is the best thing in the world."

"Does this mean we have a truce?"

"No." Molly slid one hand between Seph's thighs. "We do not have a truce. The battle will rage on, but only after I get you to scream out my name."

Chapter Nine

"Molly. You need to accept that Persephone Milan is renovating the saloon."

"Cosmo."

"What?"

"She changed her name back to Cosmo after the divorce. She said so at the town hall meeting."

Jeb ran a hand over his forehead. "Yeah. Right. Sorry. Ms. Cosmo is renovating the saloon. This is happening, Molly, and you need to accept it."

This had all started when Molly had asked her dad if he wasn't the tiniest bit concerned about Seph's plans. She was doing dishes from dinner, and her father was bustling around the kitchen in preparation for a big event in the Primrose's front room that evening. Her dad had reacted to her question with immediate defensiveness. Now they were basically in a full-blown argument.

"Why do I have to accept it? Why do any of us?"

The same bright hazel eyes she'd known all her life examined her closely. The familiar wrinkles around the edges softened her heart. "Sweetheart." He put a hand on her shoulder. The warmth and weight were as familiar as his gaze. "What is really going on with you?"

Molly let out a sigh so loud it moved the hair draped over

her forehead. "It's about the saloon. My tour. The town. All of it. She's ruining all of it."

Jeb cocked his head to one side. "I don't see how. Honey, you aren't thinking long term. I know you hate the fence and the construction. I know it's distracting for your tours. In fact, it's distracting for all the tourists. But it's still early in the season, and Persephone is working her crews double-time to finish up before the big anniversary of the showdown. I mean, to be honest, getting it done this season is a bit of a miracle, let alone by August. It looks bad now, but it will all work out in the end."

Molly stared at her father. His guileless expression nearly crumbled her resolve. But if Seph's kisses yesterday didn't do it, neither would her father's insistence today. "Dad, I know what this town needs. And even if I'm literally the only one who's willing to do what's right, I'm going to do it."

Her father pulled her to him for a warm hug. "You always do what you think is right. And I love you for it."

The embrace felt so much like all the ones they'd shared after Molly returned from Seattle, her self-confidence in tatters. Her father had held her and said things like that, reminding her of all the things she was good at, all the reasons she would be okay.

Unwilling to dredge that up again, Molly managed to extricate herself from her father. "Okay. So, what else do we need to do for this gathering tonight?"

Her father eyed her. She was pretty sure he wanted to uninvite her at this point. But there was no way Molly was missing the Q&A with Seph she'd promised at the town hall meeting. "I think we're good. We have almost an hour until it starts. Go get Etta. Have a drink before you come back." He winked at her.

Molly kissed her dad on the cheek and took the ten-minute walk to the Oasis. A crisp breeze penetrated the edges of Molly's light jacket, and by the time she burst into the pub and caught a glimpse of herself in the security mirror that hung by the door, her cheeks were rosy and her nose was pink.

"Hey." Etta greeted her from the empty bar.

Molly spread her arms. "Where is everyone?"

"At your parents' tea, probably."

"I just came from there. No one was there yet."

Etta shrugged. "You ready for this?"

"Not really."

Etta rounded the bar and stood in front of Molly. "What, exactly, is going on with you and Seph? Because I feel like it's more than you've told me."

For some reason, the thought running through Molly's head came bursting out of her. "Yesterday at this time I was giving Seph head, and now she's preparing to charm the entire town to get them to see her way, and I know that none of us stand a chance."

Etta's eyes grew wide. "Um. Wow. You wanna talk about that? The, uh, sex thing?"

"No, I don't."

She turned toward the door, but Etta jumped in front of her. "Wait. You need to back way up."

"We need to go to that meeting."

"What exactly are you going to do there?"

Molly shifted her weight to her back foot and bit her lip.

Etta stared her down. "You don't know."

"I'll figure it out on the way there."

"Better idea." Etta grasped Molly's upper arm and pulled her over to a small table near the far wall. She dropped Molly into a horrifically uncomfortable chair, grabbed a bottle of whiskey and two glasses, and took the seat opposite her. "We're going to talk this through."

Molly had to admit that it wasn't a bad idea. She did need a strategy before she barged into another situation where she ended up standing alone with a massive chip on her shoulder and no one to help lift it. She needed a plan this time. And her dad had suggested she have a drink.

She watched as Etta poured caramel-colored liquid into both glasses. "Okay. Help me strategize."

Etta pushed one glass across the table. "We're not starting there, girl."

Molly picked up the drink and took a swig. After a slight cringe as the whiskey burned on its way down her throat, she dropped the glass to the table and stared back at her best friend. "Seph and I went to UC Berkeley together."

Etta threw her head back. "What? Why didn't you tell me that?"

"I don't know. It didn't come up."

Etta raised an eyebrow.

"Because the rich techie Persephone Milan is completely separated in my mind from the Seph Cosmo I knew in school. Look, the point is, I didn't keep it from you on purpose."

"So when you say you knew her in college, what exactly do you mean?"

"She majored in history. I minored in it. We had a few class-es together. I noticed her."

Etta smirked. "I bet you did."

"She was gorgeous then, and she's stunning now."

"I've noticed."

"Anyway. We would smile at each other, and maybe say hi in passing every once in a while. Nothing more than that. We never really had a conversation. And I never saw her outside of class until the graduation party."

"You were both at the same party?"

"Yeah. And almost as soon as I walked in the door, I spotted her. She was wearing this sundress. God, I still remember it." Molly closed her eyes to savor the image.

Etta chuckled, and Molly's eyes flew open. "Anyway, she looked great. And I was going to sit there and watch her all night, but she came over to me. Walked right up to where I was."

"And she grabbed you by the hair and kissed you?"

Molly chuckled. "No, we went out to the porch and spent hours talking."

"That's not what I was expecting."

Molly dropped a hand on Etta's shoulder. "There's more."

"I hope so."

"My roommate didn't make the graduation cut. She had to come back for another semester in the fall. She was depressed about it, so she didn't stick around. She moved out a few days before the party."

"So you had the place to yourself. That's what you're saying in a ridiculously and unnecessarily detailed way."

"God, you are so impatient. Yes. That's right. So we went back to my apartment, and we talked some more and drank some more, and then we had sex."

Etta clapped her hands. "Yeah you did! Was it good?"

Molly closed her eyes. "Definitely."

"So you just did it the once?"

Molly's eyelids shot open again, and she gaped at Etta. "Are you crazy? Of course not, we did it like three or four times that night."

Etta laughed again, the sound low and rich, not unlike Seph's moans. Molly tried to push that from her mind. "I meant, did you ever see her again?"

"For a second at graduation the next day."

"And?"

Molly sighed. This was the hard part of the story. The last thing she needed was to let on to Etta how hard it was for her to remember it. "I ran into her as we were all lining up to go into the arena."

Molly had scanned the crowd. Aside from basic indications of size, everyone had looked the same. Long gowns and graduation caps had been spread out in front of her like a sea of lemmings all ready to take the plunge into the post-college world of work and responsibility.

She'd woken up that morning in a barely recognizable state. Seph was still beside her, looking like every dream come true. Naked, eyes closed, and a slight, adorable snore. It was heaven. Molly had stared at Seph for at least twenty minutes, imagining a new life for them both. They could date, even if it did have to be long-distance. There was no reason to let that stop them.

There was something here. Something big. Molly could feel it in her chest.

"Molly." That same soft, hesitant tone from the night before had punctured Molly's concentration, and she turned around to find Seph standing behind her, graduation gown draping elegantly over her form, cap slightly askew.

"Hey."

"Hey."

Molly had put her hand on Seph's waist. It was a question. An experiment.

Seph had moved closer, tipping her head. It was like she was begging for a kiss. Molly bit her lip as she debated whether or not to give it to her.

Seph's eyes sparkled with challenge. "Thanks for breakfast."

Molly grinned. She had fed Seph coffee and a muffin from the café across the street that morning. But she was pretty sure that wasn't the breakfast Seph was referring to. "My pleasure. Should we do it again?"

Seph pressed her lips against Molly's in a quick, sweet kiss. "We definitely should. But . . ." She let out a long sigh. "I have to have dinner with my parents after the ceremony."

Molly had expected as much. "Yeah, me too. But they'll probably go back to their hotel around nine-ish."

Seph smiled. "I will try to get rid of my parents and my ex by then. And maybe we can connect?"

Seph had looked so hopeful, her eyes wide. But Molly was caught up by something else Seph had said. "Your ex?"

Seph's eyes moved to the ceiling and then back to Molly. "Yeah. Apparently he came with my parents."

"Greg?"

"Yeah."

Molly's stomach ached. "But you said you were broken up."

Seph's lips slammed together in a hard line. Her fingers pressed against Molly's back. "Yes. I did. We broke up months ago."

Molly pulled her close and planted a kiss on her cheek. "I'm sorry. I didn't mean to sound accusatory. Of course you did. I just don't understand why he's here."

"Neither do I. When I went to pick up my parents at their hotel, he was standing there with them."

"But you didn't invite him?"

Seph shifted, pulling back a little. "No. I told you."

"I know. I know. I'm confused."

"My parents invited him. They don't know about everything that's happened between me and Greg, and they don't understand that it's really over between us."

"Maybe it's not over for him."

"No. It's definitely over for him. I rejected him for good, and he's not going to forgive that. Can we not talk about Greg?" Seph pushed herself closer to Molly as a voice wafted through the overhead speakers announcing that the graduates needed to prepare for the walk into the arena. The hard lines of Seph's face softened.

People had started to shuffle forward, and the sound around them grew so it was difficult to hold a conversation. Seph placed her lips beside Molly's ear. "So, we're on for tonight, right?"

A shiver ran through Molly. Seph was going to be with her, and Greg Milan was all but forgotten.

Two hours later, Molly and Seph's plans had been turned

upside down. Molly was seated with the other students in the Journalism school, separated from Seph in the vast arena, as they sat through speech after speech. But she'd had a good vantage point as Seph walked across the stage to receive her diploma.

Molly was supposed to be queuing up with her class at that moment because they'd be next to walk up the steps to the wide stage. Her seatmate had to poke her in the back to get her to stand up and weave through the narrow row of chairs.

Even as she moved into line, Molly's gaze kept flitting back to the stage. She caught Seph getting her diploma and shaking hands with the dean. But then she had to look away again to keep from stepping on Roger Bish's gown. She heard the dean speak into the microphone. He was saying something about inviting a former graduate onto the stage, and when her gaze returned, there was Greg Milan. He stood beside the dean and in front of Seph, who was stock still, her diploma still clutched in one hand.

Seph's mouth dropped open in shock as Greg knelt down on one knee in front of her. Molly turned her entire body toward the stage, not caring that her shoe caught on a chair and nearly toppled it. A quiet wave drifted over the entire arena as Greg spoke into a microphone. He was talking about Seph being beautiful and kind and smart. But Molly was focused on Seph.

She was far enough away that it was hard to see her expression. But her body was stiff, her hands clenched in fists at her sides. Molly clasped her own hands together. Seph was about to have the most humiliating experience of her life. Greg was proposing, and she'd have to say no to this man in front of everyone.

Molly wanted to run to her, scoop her up, and carry her off that stage. She'd take Seph back to her apartment and love all the hurt away.

But none of that happened.

Molly almost couldn't believe her own ears as Seph took the microphone from Greg after he'd finished his proposal. She

spoke clearly into it. Just one word. One word that had stopped
Molly's heart and turned it to a brick of frigid ice. "Yes."

Etta's eyes were wide. "I can't believe she said yes. I thought for
sure you were going to tell me she turned him down."

Molly glared at Etta from under her lashes. "Did you really
think that's how this story was going to go?"

"Seems better than she said yes because a few thousand people were watching and then actually went through with it and
had a miserable marriage for ten years, followed by a very public
divorce."

"Yeah, it would have been a better story."

Etta poured another round of whiskey. "Damn. That's
messed up."

Molly shrugged to keep the tears pricking at her eyes from
falling. "It is what it is."

"Oh, Mol. You're playing it way too cool. Don't even try with
me. It sounds like you had a broken heart all those years ago."

Molly scoffed. "Broken heart. Come on, E. It was one night.
I've had a lot more since then."

It wasn't a lie. Molly'd had a lot of lovers. But the truth she'd
never admit to anyone, not even to Etta, was that her heart had
broken that day. Her night with Seph had been special. She'd
felt the beginnings of something that had been hard to let go,
and it had been ripped from her in one horrible moment of betrayal. The moment Seph said "yes."

Etta frowned. "Sometimes it's the ones that got away that
hurt the most."

"Stop."

"So, uh." Etta twirled the glass in her hand. "Does Seph's
reappearance as the woman with all the power and money throw
shadows of Kelsy?"

"Can we please head to the meeting now?"

Etta rose slowly. "Okay. But only on the condition that you don't say a word without my permission."

"What?"

"You heard me. I'm the chip clip on your bag of self-righteous indignation. If I decide it's appropriate to let it fly, I will give you this signal." Etta pointed her finger toward Molly with her thumb up as if she were shooting an imaginary gun.

"Seriously?"

"I'm completely serious. And if you speak when I haven't given you the signal, I will stand up and announce to everyone that you once drank the better part of a fifth of vodka and then ate a massive bowl of spaghetti and thirty minutes later threw up in front of your most famous tour guest."

"You wouldn't."

"Oh, I sure as hell would, just like that guest would sing the best friggin' song about being in love with someone that is about to die."

"Fuck."

"Let's go."

The sitting room at the Primrose was packed. It was, quite literally, standing room only. In fact, it was probably a fire code violation, but the chief of the volunteer fire department was perched happily on a settee in the middle of the room next to her wife looking very engaged, so apparently no one was going to clear the room.

Etta dragged Molly to the corner of the room closest to the door. It wasn't easy to squeeze between the wall and Jeb Green's beloved Monstera plant, but Etta managed to wedge them in, her shoulder in front of Molly as if she were holding her back from running into the center of the room where Seph stood.

Seph looked particularly striking in a deep purple suit. She was quite possibly the only person to ever wear a skirt suit in the history of the town. But she was certainly pulling it off. She looked as comfortable as Molly did in a pair of jeans and an oversized hoodie.

A hint of cleavage peeked out from Seph's silky top. Her hair hung over one shoulder as if it had been purposely placed there by the most meticulous hair artist on a movie set. Her eyes shone brightly, carefully moving from one person to another as she spoke.

"I was on a tour. Not with the best tour guide in town, mind you." Seph's gaze flitted to Molly's parents, and she shot them a sly grin before turning back to Evelyn in the front row. "I loved Theia instantly, and when I saw the saloon for the first time, I was completely intrigued by its story. I immediately bought the book by the actual best tour guide in town."

A brief chuckle ran through the room and someone, though Molly couldn't tell who, finger snapped. It was also in that moment that Mayor Wright turned her head and spotted Molly. Her gaze somehow attracted that of several other people in the room. Soon most of the room was staring at her.

But she didn't see any of them. She was too busy watching Seph glance her way. Seph winked at her before turning back to the crowd and continuing. "And I consumed that book like it was junk food. I read it in one sitting, only getting up to pee and grab a drink. You know what I mean?"

Several people nodded their heads. Molly let out her breath as the attention in the room moved away from her spot in the corner and back to where Seph was holding court in the center of the room.

"And I became a little obsessed with the place. I would pull up all the photos I took that day on my tablet and zoom in so I could examine every building and especially the saloon. I examined every corner of it and found myself circling places that needed repair and X'ing out places that should be left alone and preserved as they were. My cousin's best friend, who's an architect, was at her house, where I was staying. And he saw what I was doing and decided to get involved. We came back and looked at the place together. It was a Monday, and apparently you all stay home on Mondays."

Another wave of laughter rolled through the room. "Anyway, we popped into the Primrose to see if we could find someone who'd let us into some of the locked buildings, and we found Jeb."

Molly loved her father. He was undeniably a good man. But in that moment, her father's betrayal stung. He had kept this all from her for far longer than she knew. She glanced at him, and he caught her eye. But she looked away, refocusing on Seph. Molly would have to deal with Jeb Green later.

"We were able to look at the place closely and make concrete plans. That night I called Stan and made him that now famous offer. And I admit that at first, my plans were not perfect. I majored in history in college, but I never worked as a historian. I had grand plans that didn't fit the need. I understand that now, and I'm humbled by all your help." Seph waved her hand across the room. "So now, with your support, I'm going to begin a comprehensive preservation project in Theia, one that preserves the character of the ghost town and highlights its legendary past."

Seph moved back a step until she stood beside an easel. It was the same one that Janet kept on the porch for visiting artists. Seph gently removed a white sheet from the easel to reveal a drawing. Molly imagined Seph would rather have projected the image on a large screen television, but the Primrose didn't have one. Instead, she gestured to the drawing with pride.

"This plan calls for meticulous restoration of every one of the twenty-two buildings in the proposed park, with some being in working order. The Warsaw and the blacksmith shop for sure, and we're talking about possibly restoring the original general store and making that an extension of Evelyn's store with limited merchandise. At any rate, Janet and Jeb have agreed to leave this up in the front room of the Primrose for the next few days so you can all look it over at your leisure."

Molly's mother moved from her place at the edge of the room toward Seph. "Thank you so much, Persephone." She flashed her kindest smile before turning toward the room. "Now we're ready for some questions. Please raise your hand, and I will call on you one at time. Who would like to go first?"

Molly could feel a dozen pairs of eyes boring into her, almost as if they were daring her to speak. But they must know, as she did, that Janet Green would never invite that level of chaos into an event she organized.

"Hadley, yes. What's your question, dear?"

Hadley Rivers was the darling of Theia. She was the first baby born in Montana in the new millennium. Her parents lived in an old Victorian they had fixed up just after getting married. Her dad was an obstetrician at Bozeman's hospital, but Hadley wasn't born in Bozeman. She was in too much of a hurry, and her father had delivered her right there in Theia, a fact that made all the papers. So she was already the town's favorite child when she announced at the age of twelve during a town council meeting that she was a girl, and she wanted everyone to start treating her like a girl.

Molly couldn't remember the bigots now, but she did know there had been a few. They were overwhelmed, however, by the small-town love and support that poured out for Hadley. Four years later, Molly came out, albeit in a slightly less public way, and two years after that Etta moved to town to live with and work for her uncle after getting into trouble in the big city of Billings. That same year Burt and Kevin moved in and fixed up the Meyer mansion which sat on the other side of the future park area from the Primrose. The two regal buildings flanked it like sentries, there to guard it through time. Burt and Kevin had turned the mansion into a successful wedding venue. And last year Mauve and Clinton, the fire chief and her wife, who owned an online business, had moved into town.

Hadley had paved the way for them all, making Theia the queer haven it was now. She deserved the town adoration she was the recipient of. And having graduated with honors from an Ivy League school then returning to the area to work in the finance department for the county didn't hurt either.

Whatever Hadley had to say would carry a lot of weight, and everyone in the room knew it. From the look on her face, Seph knew it too.

"I was wondering, Ms. Cosmo."

"Seph, please."

Hadley flashed her million-watt smile, and a tinge of what had to be jealousy hit Molly in the chest.

"Seph, I love your ideas and your heart, but I'm wondering about the economics of your proposal."

Molly threw her head back and squeezed her eyes shut to keep her celebration as hidden as possible. This was exactly what she needed—the smartest person in the room to challenge Seph on the realities of her plan. When she opened her eyes again, Seph was smiling back at Hadley in a way that was way too sweet. Molly's jealousy ramped up.

Hadley stood. "The thing is, I look at numbers all day. And I know that over eighty percent of every dollar that comes into this town comes in between May and September. The entire town has to live off that for the other seven months of the year. Some businesses close for the winter, like the restaurant. And Kyle heads to Arizona by early October." Hadley shot Kyle, who sat near her in a folding chair, a glance. "Not that we blame you."

Kyle laughed. "I hate winter."

"And honestly," Hadley continued, "it's smart. There are virtually no tourists in the winter except for a handful of hunters over a few weeks. And none of the landowners let them hunt on their property, so they buy a few things, or spend one night at the bed-and-breakfast so they can get a shower and a hot meal. Then they go on their way. My point is: what is your plan in terms of being open? Because, I'll be honest, I'm part of a group trying to push for more commerce in the winter months, or at the very least the fall and spring. And if you close off the most famous spot in town for over half the year, I'm not sure our campaign will stand a chance."

Molly wanted to run across the room and kiss Hadley directly on the mouth. For the first time since this all started, she finally felt like someone was in her corner. And it happened to be the most revered person in town. Hadley hadn't been at the town council meeting, and Molly had allowed herself to feel defeated after that disaster. But this was a whole new game now. The tides were changing before her very eyes.

Seph's smile didn't falter as she kept her attention on Hadley, who lowered herself back onto the couch between Stan and Jenny Fine. "I hear you. I am, at my core, a businesswoman. Even if my passion for history sits on my heart."

Molly leaned over to whisper to Etta. "See. When she talks like that she sounds like a salesman not a historian."

Etta shushed her. "She has a degree in history."

Molly rolled her eyes but kept her mouth shut.

Seph continued, her gaze locked on Hadley. "I've run the numbers. And I know you'll get this, given your job and your extreme talent with numbers. It was bleak at first. I ran a year-round model. And as you pointed out, in the model I lost all the money I earned in the summer during the winter months."

Molly could feel the wave of dissent hovering over this room. She was so grateful she hadn't missed this.

"However . . ." Seph held up her hand. "That was only for the first year. So I ran it for the second, third, and fourth years. They were slightly better each year, but not enough. Then I ran projections on the fifth year with the variables that the rest of the town stays open. And you know what I found? By year five, the town becomes a year-round attraction. We bring in skiers headed to Bozeman in the winter and Yellowstone traffic in the fall and spring. We get the newlyweds and retirees vacationing on the edges of the season to avoid the families. And we turn a profit year-round. All of us."

The room went ominously still.

Etta whispered, "Holy shit."

Molly could feel the momentum slipping through her hands. She had to think of something that could put a hard stop to this stump-like speech.

But someone else came to her rescue. Kyle stood. "May I?"

Seph waved her hand. "Please."

"With all due respect, Ms. Cosmo."

"Please, call me Seph."

"Seph. You have the bank account to lose money for five years. The rest of us don't. I don't run to Arizona and sun myself. I operate a business down there as well. I can't afford to lose money for seven months of the year for five years. None of us can. It takes money to stay open and empty."

"And . . ." Dale raised his hand even as he spoke. Tucked into the corner near the fireplace, still wearing his forest service uniform, Dale was an opposing figure, even seated. "Someone has to staff the old buildings. We've got security and safety to look after as well as demonstrations at the blacksmith shop. And if you really want more tourists, you'll need more demonstrations, people in costume, more tours. Molly's are high-end specialty tours, and that woman from Bozeman only brings people twice a week. You'll need daily tours. We all take turns volunteering in the summer, but if you want to keep it open in the winter, that means hiring people."

"I can do that." Seph's words echoed through the room. "I will pay for staff, and to house the people who come in. I've bought the old miner bachelors' quarters behind the Oasis from Kyle."

Seph gestured with her chin to Kyle, who merely nodded. So that was the deal he was so tight-lipped about the other day. Damn.

"The bones on that building are good," Seph said. "If I renovated it, I think it could make ten modern studio apartments. That could help attract people to work at the park. And as for the years of losses, I can help with that too. I spoke to Mayor Wright about setting up a small-business fund to draw from. What do you think?"

It all sounded too good to be true. Especially the part about the bachelors' quarters. Everyone in town could use a helping hand. Her parents busted their butts to keep the Primrose running. The store hours were limited by Evelyn's time and how bad her arthritis was on any given day. Kyle was always stretched thin, especially when all his staff except Etta went back to college in the fall. And housing was a big part of the problem.

And the bachelors' quarters was the one building in town Molly wouldn't cry over if it burned to the ground. It was ugly, and so was its history. It was like a dark cloud perched on the hillside above the restaurant. It was the first thing anyone saw when they drove into town, and every tourist asked about it. Molly hated that building, and she had no heart to try to keep Seph from doing whatever she wanted to it. In that one case, there was no way to ruin it. Seph must have known that. Jeb had probably told her. And now Seph had thrown new ammunition into their fight.

Chapter Ten

Gravel crunched under Molly's feet as she headed toward the back of the old inn. Her father and a handful of other residents had filled in the town's original dump site with gravel to keep tourists from tripping on the soft, rotted soil, and now it was incredibly loud. She left the dump and turned left toward the back door of the inn.

It was one of Molly's favorite places. Like a secret cove, it was hidden and quiet. She paused outside the staff door. This nondescript entrance made of sturdy wood and once painted white, the remnants of which still clung to it in a few places, hinted at what it must have looked like in its day.

The white would have blended in with the walls of the building, not like the bright red doors at the main entrance that welcomed guests to the regal hotel. This door was meant to hide the transformation of a person whose real life was undesirable to the wealthy guests into the smiling employee who carried their bags or served them coffee.

This was her spot now. A century and a half after those unnamed servants used this door as a gateway to change from whoever their real selves were into people-pleasing customer servants, she used it to put on her persona before a tour.

It had been easier lately. When she first came to Theia, Molly hated her life. She hated that she'd run back home after an epic failure. She despised the image of herself as a tour guide that sucked up to people who were living the life she wanted to live. Every time someone asked what degree she was studying for in college or what she wanted to be when she grew up, she nearly vomited.

It took a while to get used to the common assumption that only a person in transition would give tours of a ghost town. It was during a trip to Yellowstone that she had her "aha" moment. She was taking a tour of one of the geyser basins with a park ranger. At the end of the tour, the ranger asked if people had questions. She got hit with a familiar one for Molly. "What are you going to do after this?"

The ranger squared her shoulders and said, "I graduated summa cum laude from a well-respected university. Then I immediately took an internship with the park service. Three years later, I am here with you people. I imagine in three more years I might be lead. After that, maybe a supervisor. Who knows. But here's the thing: this is my career. I chose it. I love it. And I'm good at it."

That speech had sunk into Molly's chest and stayed there, slowly working on her. She used to stand here behind the inn, ready to give a tour, and think about the way Kelsy dismissed her at the magazine. And then she would pull up the image of that ranger, straighten her back, and march out to meet them.

Things were different these days. People booked her tours because they knew who she was. They'd read her stories or seen her speak, or watched one of the documentaries she was featured in. And nowadays, before she gave a tour, she didn't think about Kelsy or her stupid magazine. She didn't linger too long on the ranger either. Instead, she thought about her role in this historic place and how it had shifted from being another person using it to make a living to being its champion, its protector. This place had saved her when she'd nearly drowned herself, and now she was saving it.

Molly stepped away from the peeling wall. Her gaze was pointed in the direction of the spot where her tour group would be meeting her in a few moments when she heard a sound.

She turned so quickly her feet made a pattern in the dirt. She searched for the source, her eyes darting around the dusty ground and sparse brush. Movement snagged her roving gaze, which landed on a tiny white ball of fluff.

As soon as she spotted it, the little dog noticed her as well. It moved toward her, tail wagging. It yipped as it approached, but the sound wasn't threatening. If anything it was comical.

Molly dropped down to her knees, prepared to wait for the pup to cautiously approach her. But there was no pause for stranger danger in this little one's demeanor. It rushed toward her and leaped into her arms.

All six or so pounds of the puppy wiggled and climbed up her chest until its tiny tongue could reach out and lick her chin. "Hey there. Who are you?"

Molly attempted to read the small metal tag hanging from a pink collar. But between the copious quantity of thick, fluffy fur and the constant motion, it proved impossible. She was, however, able to determine that her new friend was a girl dog. So at least she had the correct pronoun now.

"Hey, girl. Where did you come from?"

The pup was in very good shape—well-groomed, and not the least bit dirty, which was pretty remarkable because even fifteen minutes on the dirt streets of Theia should have had her covered in a layer of dust.

"Oh my god, you found her!" Seph rounded the corner of the hotel and bounded toward Molly, arms outstretched. Before Molly could even react, Seph had scooped the dog out of her hands and was pressing her against her neck. "Oh baby, don't scare me like that!"

Molly stood, casually brushing off her pants. "You have a dog?"

With her gaze still pinned to the pup, Seph responded. "Yes. This is Belle." She patted Belle's head affectionately.

"Your small, fluffy dog is named Belle? That checks out."

"She's fierce. Which is why her full name is Belle Starr."

"Oh." Somehow it was way cooler to have the dog named after a famous female outlaw of the Old West.

Seph peered at Molly over the top of Belle's head. "Nothing I ever do is good enough for you, is it?"

Molly held up her hands. "Hey, I didn't say anything."

Seph let out a harrumph that might have been a very unattractive sound on anyone else. On her it was more like a sexy moan.

"Why didn't I see Belle at the B&B the other day?"

"She was staying with my cousin until I got the house ready enough for us to move in. But that's going to take a while, and I really missed her. So your parents said she could stay at the Primrose."

Her parents loved dogs, but they'd had too many guests that were allergic. So with the exception of service dogs, they had barred all pets. Apparently though, as with all things, Seph got her way. Molly wondered if she had any idea how much privilege she wielded in this tiny town.

"Well, that's nice. Try to keep her from running away, though. It's dangerous around here." Molly pointed in the direction of the Warsaw. "Someone has a construction site over there."

Seph glared at her.

"Well, I gotta go give a tour—you know, minus the most famous site in town."

"Do you have room?"

"What?"

Seph spoke more slowly. "Do you have room on your tour?"

"Why? You don't need one. You already had a tour with the great Shannon McGregor."

Seph rolled her eyes. "My cousin is here. She came to drop off Belle. And I think she'd enjoy it. Do you have room?"

Her tour today was not a private one. Instead, she'd combined several couples who'd shown interest in taking her tour, but didn't have the required ten-person minimum. So, yeah, she could totally take Seph's cousin. That didn't mean she wanted to. Still, she sighed and nodded.

Seph's eyes lit up, and she gave out a little yelp of delight that Molly thought was an overblown reaction to such a simple thing. "She's around here somewhere helping me look for Belle." She lifted her head and belted out, "*Kaaaarrrraaaa!*"

A faint voice returned what Molly could barely make out. "Did you find her?"

"I found her. Come here. By the old hotel."

The sound of Kara's voice was closer now. "Which one is the old hotel?"

"Dude. It's the one that looks like a hotel."

Molly couldn't help but laugh at the unexpected irreverence coming from Persephone Milan herself.

A woman came into view from the opposite direction. She wore a dark blue flannel shirt, jeans, and the same brand of boots Molly wore. Her straight brown hair was tied back in a loose ponytail and had none of the bounce or shine of Seph's locks.

"Hey. There you are. Hey, Belle, you silly girl. Don't run off like that." She booped the dog's nose before turning to Molly. "Oh, hi. I'm Kara. Seph's cousin." She held out a hand devoid of any manicure whatsoever.

Molly shook her hand. "Molly Green."

"Molly rescued Belle."

"Not really. It was she who found me. Anyway." Molly swung her head toward the sign Mayor Wright had erected to indicate visitors had reached the oldest part of Theia. She could see that at least four people had already gathered there. She hated that. She always liked to be standing there when all her tour guests arrived. "I gotta go."

"Kara," Seph said. "Molly said you can join her tour."

"Really? Awesome."

Molly turned to walk away, and Kara kept stride. "This is great. Thanks."

"Have fun," Seph called.

Molly tried to push aside all the contradictions that were Seph Cosmo and focus on her tour group, but they would not fully go away. She had a feeling the same thing went for the woman herself. She'd embedded herself in Theia like a burr in a dog's fur, and she'd done the same to Molly's life.

Kara was cool. No two ways about it. She was respectful during the tour, but also very funny. It was a rare guest who could inject funny comments without being either overly cheesy or a raging asshole. Kara was that rarity.

Molly waved one last goodbye to the guests before walking away with Kara beside her. "Maybe we should team up. Together we'd have them eating out of the palms of our hands."

Kara's stride nearly matched Molly's. "You already had them eating out of your hand. You don't need me; you're a stone-cold professional."

Molly laughed. "We could charge even more. Come to the bar with me?" She turned down Thimble Street.

"Definitely. And don't tempt me to join you as a co-guide. The kids would miss me."

"How many?"

"Three. When Ryan got the Division One coaching job, we decided I could do the stay-at-home thing. I jumped at the chance. My job as an admin in the financial aid office at the last college we were at bored me to tears."

"But the mom thing doesn't?" Molly caught herself. "I mean

. . . I didn't mean to be rude. I don't have any kids or nieces or nephews, and the whole thing seems kind of unpleasant to me."

Kara stopped in her tracks, threw her head back, and let out a massive gut laugh. "Oh wow. You sound exactly like Seph."

"I do?"

Kara wiped at her eyes and started moving again. Molly touched her arm lightly and steered her toward the back entrance of the Oasis. She considered asking more questions about Seph and her apparent dislike of children. Instead, she pointed to the bar. "This is currently Theia's only bar. It's not much, but it's ours." That was Kyle and Etta's favorite saying about the bar. It stuck in Molly's mind and rolled around for a second. This quaint local tradition was about to come to an end thanks to Seph.

"In we go then." Kara swung the door open and gestured for Molly to go first. Molly was usually the one holding the door for other women, but she didn't object. She ducked inside to find Rosie catapulting toward her and Etta greeting them from behind the bar.

"Hey Mol! Who'd you bring in?"

Kara stopped at the entrance and looked around. There was absolutely no one in here today other than them. "This is good. Different, but good. I had no idea such a thing as an empty bar existed in Montana."

Etta wasn't the least bit offended. She and Kara introduced themselves and shook hands. As Kara slipped onto a barstool, Etta hooked her thumb over her shoulder. "Restaurant's packed though."

As if he'd been conjured, Jeff came flying through the open doorway that led to a hall connecting the restaurant's dining room, kitchen, and bar. He gave a few orders, and Kara and Molly waited until Etta was free again.

"Post-tour drink?" Etta asked.

"Please."

"I'm intrigued. Whatever it is, make it two," Kara said.

"Good tour or bad tour?" Etta asked.

"Good tour."

Etta moved to mix Molly her usual drink. "Even with Seph's fence in your way?"

Molly cringed. "I think I forgot to mention that Kara is Seph's cousin."

Kara laughed while Etta did her best to look contrite. "Sorry."

Kara waved her hand. "Don't worry. I know all about the feud."

Etta returned to fixing the drinks. "It's pretty interesting, isn't it?"

"Oh yeah. Especially given their history."

Molly nearly fell off her barstool. What did Kara know? How much had Seph told her?

Etta seemed every bit as shocked. She placed both drinks on the bar and leaned over, her arms spread wide across the old wooden surface. "Yeah. I just found out about that myself."

"I heard about it back when it happened."

Molly supposed Seph had to have someone to talk to after she slept with a woman the night before she got engaged to a man. Kara seemed like the perfect person to talk to.

"Is that right?" Etta asked.

Kara nodded. "It was a big deal."

"I bet it was. Tell me more."

"Not too much to tell. They weren't a thing after that. But the minute Seph realized she and Molly Green were squaring off in the same tiny town, she told me about that one night all over again."

Molly took a long swig of her drink. It was smooth, which was exactly the way she liked her "good tour" drink. She left the harsh stuff for the "bad tour" drink. She desperately wanted to ask Kara if she knew about their frantic and unexpected hot sex in the bed-and-breakfast the other day. But that might open a door she wouldn't be able to shut. Best to pretend that never happened until confronted with absolute proof.

"Okay. So. Next subject," Molly announced. "Let's talk tiny dogs." She patted Rosie on the head. "Etta, you'll never guess what Kara brought to town today."

Etta and Kara gave in and let her have her topic shift. They happily discussed Rosie and Belle and speculated about whether they would be friends or enemies if they met. But Molly never fully relaxed into the conversation. Her flings with Seph, now numerous, weighed on her. If she couldn't forget them, she'd have to find some other way to incorporate their memories into her current reality, a reality that pitted Seph and her against one another in an epic battle for Theia.

Chapter Eleven

Molly grinned with satisfaction at the text from Seph.

Why is my social media blowing up?

It was Seph's second text message after getting Molly's number from her mom. The first had been sent three days ago to inform Molly that Seph now had her number and that her mother wanted her to come to dinner that night.

The dinner was one that everyone at the Primrose was invited to. Her father liked to say that the Primrose was a "bed-and-breakfast and sometimes dinner." Seph and Molly ended up on opposite ends of the long rectangular table in the dining room. Afterward, when her parents and the guests headed to the parlor for after-dinner coffee and tea, Molly and Seph had snuck up to the Georgette for a quickie.

Now, Seph's text was reminding Molly about the online attack she had started on Seph last week. She'd completely forgotten about it since her post had initially fizzled out without gaining much traction. This morning, for some unknown reason, the historical preservation warriors had picked it back up.

Oops.

It's too late to stop me now, Molly. Just give it up.

Who says it's too late?

Why don't you take a drive toward Bozeman. Turn around at Four Corners and head back. Keep your eyes peeled.

What the hell did that mean? Molly's gaze roamed from her phone out the window of the cabin where she could see her car parked on the rutted strip that ran along the lesser-used side of the Primrose.

It was the middle of the afternoon. She was supposed to be at her desk working on the fourth book in the Theia series. Instead, she'd been lying across the couch doom-scrolling on her phone when the text came in. Since that was a perfectly reasonable activity to interrupt for a random drive, she got up and grabbed her keys.

Twenty minutes later, keys still clutched in her hand, Molly stormed into the Primrose like a hurricane. One of the matching double doors slammed against her mother's antique table. The tiny, spindly thing, barely big enough to hold a small purse or wallet, stayed upright in defiance of her anger.

Her mother, however, was not so unaffected. "Molly, what the hell?"

Molly pointed her finger at Seph, who sat primly on the settee with Belle tucked into her lap. An older couple sat across from her. They paused in mid-motion. The one man had the tea cup halfway to his mouth; the other held his hovering over the saucer. Their eyes were as wide open as the front doors now were.

"We need to talk."

Seph stood slowly, carefully deposited Belle into Janet's arms, and moved toward Molly. "Then let's go somewhere a little more private." Without pausing in front of Molly she moved past her and headed to the stairs. Molly followed.

Seph calmly ushered Molly into her room, shut the door, and slipped by her, heading to the espresso machine.

"How dare you!" Molly flung her keys onto the hardwood floor. Sadly, because of the way they landed just right on the canvas key chain that read "I shot Bub Roy," they did nothing more than flop lazily without the dramatics she so desperately needed in this moment.

Seph turned to face Molly. "How dare *I*? You're the one who sicced every historian with a social media account on *me*." Seph jammed her finger into her own chest as she leaned toward Molly.

"I was trying to do the right thing. You, on the other hand . . ." Molly jammed her finger toward Seph in the same gesture without quite making contact. "Put up a billboard on the freaking highway announcing the opening day of the Warsaw Saloon." That the chosen day was August 22 was brilliant, as that was the anniversary of the day of the great showdown. Molly wasn't about to admit that.

Seph folded her arms over her chest and smirked. "Actually, it announces the *re*-opening day of the Warsaw Saloon. But you would know that if you could see the tastefully done advertisement through the fog of your misplaced anger."

It was almost impossible for Molly to imagine a more infuriating conversation. Heat was the predominant element catching her attention. It was in her boiling blood, her head full of steam, and perhaps, most predominantly, rising in her now fully activated libido. She warred with the dual concepts of stalking out of the room, and shoving Seph against a wall and kissing her until she shut up.

"My anger is *not* misplaced. It's . . . it's . . ." Her mind seemed to flutter beneath the fire pressing down on her.

"Self-righteous," Seph suggested.

"No. Righteous. Period. I. Am. Right. And You. Are. Wrong. It is absolutely beyond me how a person as smart as yourself cannot see that clearly."

"I see very clearly, Molly Green. I see a person who is completely unwilling to give someone—who might have an inkling of an idea that is the minutest difference from what you stubbornly believe to be the truth with a capital fucking T—the benefit of the doubt. You haven't changed a bit."

Molly's jaw dropped. The last thing she expected was a reference to the past. "What?"

"You heard me."

"You didn't even know me before."

Seph's face scrunched up in an expression Molly absolutely couldn't read. "I knew you well enough to know that you wouldn't bother to see what you didn't want to see."

"Seriously. What the hell does that even mean?"

Seph bit her lip as if she were deciding something. Her gaze fell to the floor. "You didn't call me."

The heat pulsed. Molly could barely breathe through its intensity. She took in a deep breath. Then another. At first, her voice was quiet and hoarse. "I couldn't." Then the heat gave her fire. "I literally watched you get engaged the next day."

She expected Seph to look guilty. Maybe even turn away. Instead, she stared straight into Molly's eyes. "I sent a text. I tried to explain. You didn't respond."

Molly glared at Seph. There were so many things unsaid between them, all begging to be let out. She wasn't even sure where to start. "Why?"

"Why did I say yes?"

Molly knew it wasn't her place to ask. What had they been but one night? She didn't have any claim on Seph back then. They hadn't declared their undying love for one another. But she couldn't help it. She nodded.

Seph let out a breath. "You know what I always tell people? I say 'it's complicated.' It's like a mantra. I use it because it's too hard to admit the truth. You deserve the truth." Seph dropped onto the bed, and Molly sat beside her. "When Greg and I started dating, on like the third or fourth date or something, we had this conversation about starting a company. We were both so excited. It was like a fire, and every sentence was fuel. The idea of the start-up was intoxicating. It grew a passion I would not have otherwise felt for him."

Seph looked down at her hands as they twisted in her lap. "We dated for two years while we were in college. We built the company in our spare time. It was our whole world. We were also determined to finish school. Since Greg was a year ahead of me, he graduated first. The deal had always been that he would work on the company full-time for that year, and I'd join him as soon as I graduated."

Seph looked up at Molly, her eyes wet. "I was so stupid. That entire year Greg was wooing investors and hiring engineers, and they all saw his face. When I showed up to meetings with a room full of guys—and they were all guys—they acted as if I wasn't even there. Greg didn't have a single investor or hire a single person that wasn't a cis white man."

"That sounds like a hard environment for you."

"It was. And I realized that no matter how dedicated I thought I was to the company, it wasn't what I wanted to build. So I made a plan to take my half in stocks and hopefully some cash and go off on my own. I wanted to find female-focused angel investors and hire young BIPOC and queer engineers, and support girls in tech programs."

"I love that."

"So did I. I loved the idea. But when I told Greg, he said that I couldn't get anything out of the company. It was all in his name. And the investors were loyal to him. I thought that was bullshit. They knew me. They knew how involved I was. So I went to each one. And they said the same thing. They were sorry, but they would be sticking with Greg."

"That's fucked up."

"I had this massive meltdown. I went to his house and cried and screamed and threw an epically embarrassing tantrum." She heaved another breath, and Molly reached over to place her hand on Seph's knee. Seph glanced at the hand, covered it with her own, and turned back to Molly. "He said that if I married him, he would make sure half of everything was mine, and he'd let me have full rein on hiring engineers and starting any kind of STEM program I wanted."

"Wait. I'm confused about the timeline."

"This was three months before graduation, almost to the day."

Molly nodded. Things were clicking into place for her. Seph held such sadness inside her the night they were together. It had been palpable. Molly was starting to understand why. She couldn't imagine carrying around that kind of stress at their age. Molly had been worried about how to get her favorite chair from Berkeley to Seattle, not the future of an entire company. "Go on."

"I said no. And I spent every day of the next three months regretting it. Every day except the one I spent with you." Seph squeezed Molly's hand. "And I'm sorry that one day wasn't enough. Maybe if it had been a week or a month. But I couldn't bet my entire future on it. So when he asked again at graduation, I said yes." She blinked and a tear fell down her cheek.

Molly lifted her hand and wiped away the tear. "Of course you did. You had to."

"You understand?"

"I never judged you for your decision, Seph. I hated what it meant for me."

Seph leaned forward, bringing her lips to Molly's, her breath fanning Molly's face. Molly's heart was racing like it was trying to beat Usain Bolt on the track.

Seph pulled back and raised the hand she had over Molly's. She touched her finger to her own neck. Molly's gaze followed that digit as it traced the neckline of her cotton blouse. Without saying a word, Seph fisted the material and pulled it straight up over her head.

The light green garment fluttered to the floor. Molly willed her eyes to stay pinned to the shirt and attempted to convince her body to rise from the bed. Now was not the time for this. There was too much happening between them. Surely it would be healthier if they worked out their past and hashed out the future before falling back into bed again. But her body stayed put.

Seph leaned over and placed a soft, gentle kiss on Molly's lips. And everything turned upside down. Seph stood up and moved in front of Molly, her fingers hooked into the hips of her leggings. Then Seph tugged, and the soft cotton slid down her thighs, hit her knees, and dropped to the ground. She stepped out of the pants with nearly unbelievable grace and slid onto Molly's lap, her legs wrapping around Molly.

Molly's hand moved to the back of Seph's neck while the other grasped her waist. Seph let out a very audible moan as she sank into Molly's grasp. Molly swallowed it. She kissed Seph with a measure of control she knew Seph loved.

Her hand drifted down to cup Seph's ass even as she rolled them both onto the bed so that Seph lay beneath her. Molly pulled her lips away from Seph and grinned. Seph was wrecked, her eyes glazed, her lips pink and moist.

Then Molly moved away in one fluid motion until she was standing at the end of the bed, staring down at Seph. She felt like a pot boiling over on the stove. There was too much inside her in this moment. She needed to find a way to control it. She hit Seph with her most serious gaze. "You're going to do exactly as I say."

Seph licked her lips.

"Take everything off."

Without answering in words, Seph did as she was told. Molly watched in awe as she discarded her bra and panties and splayed herself out on the bed, completely naked. Molly bit her lip and steadied her pounding heart before placing one knee on the bed. The mattress dipped, causing Seph's body to shift toward her.

Seph's voice was soft. "What do you want me to do?"

Molly swung one leg over so she straddled Seph's waist. She bent down and kissed a trail from her clavicle to her chin. "I want you to lie perfectly still until I tell you to move. Okay?"

Seph squeezed her eyes closed. "Okay."

Molly dropped a kiss on her lips. "Palms down."

Seph flipped her hands so they lay on the bed just as Molly wanted. Molly rewarded her by kissing the back of each hand before hovering her mouth above the part of Seph that lay between them.

Seph's breath was rough and ragged. It echoed through the room and filled Molly's ears as if it were the sound coming from a massive amplifier in a concert hall. It was all-consuming.

Molly latched onto that sound, determined to make it morph into moans and screams. She ran one hand up Seph's thigh, reveling in the silky skin beneath her palm. She moved slowly until she reached Seph's folds. She hovered there, using her fingers to play until Seph began to writhe.

Only then did she dip her head and very gently touch Seph's clit with the the tip of her wet tongue. Seph's entire body vibrated. Her throat emitted a low, cascading sound that built up into a crescendo as Molly increased her ministrations, sucking and licking with greater speed and enthusiasm.

The first orgasm hit Seph with force. But the second was the one that really did it for Molly. She pressed her fingers into Seph's thighs and held her there as she created another, more powerful wave crashing through her.

A light breeze hit Molly's cheek. The other side of her face rested on Seph's stomach. A warm, soft place she'd be happy never to leave.

Seph's fingers massaged her scalp and sifted through her short, fine hair. "I always loved your hair."

"Why?"

"It's so soft, like a baby's."

Molly snorted. "A baby. Really?"

Seph gave her head a soft tap. "You know what I mean."

Seph went back to massaging her scalp, coaxing a moan from Molly. "You really like my hair?"

"Hmmm. Hmmm. It's short, but soft and gentle. I don't know. I'm not making sense."

Molly chuckled. "It's hard to make sense post-sex."

"Hmmm. Agreed."

"Can I ask you a question?"

Seph didn't immediately respond, so Molly lifted her head and peered at her. Seph bit her lip and gazed back at Molly. "Um. I'm scared to say yes."

"It's not about *that*."

Seph let out a long breath. "Okay then."

"Do you like having sex with men as much as with women? I mean, is it equal for you, or do you like one better than the other?" Molly tucked her head back into Seph's stomach. "Maybe that's a stupid question. Or inappropriate, or whatever."

Seph's fingers resumed their work on her scalp. "It's fine, Molly. I don't mind talking about being bi."

"Okay. Cool."

"I'm definitely bi or pan or whatever. I'm attracted to people from all genders. But I've only been with men and women, and I like having sex with both. To be honest, I enjoy sex with women a bit more."

Molly lifted her head, propped herself up on her elbows and stared back at Seph. "Yeah?"

A bright blush colored Seph's cheeks. "Yeah."

"So, you've been with other women. I mean, of course. I mean, how many? Can I ask?"

"Three. You were the last before I married Greg. What about you?"

"Only women."

Seph slapped her lightly on the bicep. "You already told me you're a lesbian with no history with men that night at the party."

"Oh yeah. I forgot we had that conversation that night."

"I didn't."

"So you really want to know how many women? Hardly seems fair. It's the same as my all-persons' number and you didn't give me yours."

"Five. Two guys, three women. Everyone but Greg, and you I guess, was in my senior year of high school or my freshman year of college. Now spill."

"What if it's a lot."

"So what?"

"Yeah?"

"Yeah, really."

"My best guess is around thirty."

Seph's jaw dropped.

"I knew this was a bad idea."

Seph took a moment to compose herself. Her brow smoothed, jaw closed, eyes blinked. "No. It's fine. It's just . . ."

"More than you expected."

"Um, yeah."

"Like a lot more?"

"Kinda, yeah."

"I was pretty busy in college. And to be honest since then as well. Even here in Theia. I'm kinda irresistible to all the femme queers who take my tour. I'm not shy about offering back room special services if you know what I mean." Molly wiggled her eyebrows.

"Yeah. I definitely do."

"Does that bother you?"

"No. I just . . ."

"Don't like the idea that I might take Nan, the librarian getting a private tour, home with me tomorrow."

Seph's jaw dropped again. Molly couldn't help but laugh. "I won't. I promise. It's either a one-night stand or it's not. And as we've already established, this is more than once. So I won't mess around for as long as this keeps happening."

Something flashed across Seph's face that Molly couldn't decipher. Then she seemed to school her features, and she grinned. "Well, if you'd quit picking fights with me, it wouldn't be a problem."

Molly pressed a kiss to Seph's belly button. "I don't think it's really a problem at all." Before they could delve any further into that forbidden subject, she kissed a path down, and before long Seph was too busy moaning to say anything else.

Chapter Twelve

This coffee date meant more to Molly than she was willing to admit. In the offseason, she and her parents did this most nights of the week. But since the tourist season and her battle with Seph over the Warsaw had started, they hadn't done it once.

Molly cradled her mug in her hands and smiled at her mother. "See, this works."

Her mother's gaze roamed over Molly's cabin. "It's different than the Primrose parlor. I think I can guess the reason for the change of venue."

Molly ignored that and looked at the clock that hung over the door, because that was the only wall space available for it. "Is Dad coming?"

Her mother patted her hand. "He's coming. Of course he is. He had a last-minute thing to handle with a guest, but he'll be here in a sec."

Molly eyed her mother suspiciously. There was already something so wrong about her dad coming to this family coffee date separate from her mom, and the vague excuse her mother was giving only heightened her unease.

Things had not been right between them, and that was exactly why Molly had proposed this gathering. Growing up as an only child, Molly's parents had been her best friends, her playmates, her constant companions. And that had been especially true when they moved to Theia. At the time, they were literally the only family with kids in that first wave of about fifteen people. She was the single child in the whole town.

So, yeah, she'd been tight with her parents. Really tight. And after she returned from Seattle with her hat in her hands and her heart stomped into oblivion, their closeness had only increased. Now Jeb and Janet were more than her parents; they were her friends.

But somehow Seph Cosmo was threatening that.

"Is Dad mad at me?"

"Honey, that's ridiculous."

Molly cocked her head. "Is it? Apparently, he's been a champion of Seph's plan to buy Stan's property and renovate the saloon from the beginning—way earlier than I realized actually—and I've done everything I can to thwart those plans. And we haven't talked about any of it."

Her mother sighed. "He's not mad. He feels guilty."

Molly's mind raced. What else had her father done to aid and abet Seph? "Guilty? Why?"

"When he showed Persephone around the grounds that day, he had no idea it would turn into this. And when he voted to approve her plans—"

"Hey there." Her father popped open the cabin door, stuck his head through the opening, and they spoke all at once.

"Dad. Hi."

"Hi, honey. We were—"

"Talking about me. I know. This door is pretty thin." Jeb moved into the room.

"You want coffee?" Molly held up her mug.

"Only if it's decaf. Gotta sleep." It was the same thing her father always said when someone offered him a coffee after 1 p.m.

Jeb settled onto the small couch beside Janet while Molly took the few steps over to the kitchen and poured him a cup of coffee with one lump of sugar, the way he liked it. She handed her dad the mug and settled in the chair opposite her parents. "So you had a thing with a guest?"

Jeb took a long, slurping sip of his coffee, set the mug on the end table, and stared at Molly with the same light brown eyes she had. "Not exactly. I was having a business meeting."

"A business meeting?"

"Molly, surely you know the Primrose isn't our only source of income."

"Of course I know that." Molly was insulted that her father somehow thought that all the years she and her mother had commuted to Bozeman every day so she could go to school and her mother could teach were magically wiped from her mind.

"I mean, your mom wants to retire soon, and I have a lot of side gigs, but I'm becoming tired of having so many."

Her father was a jack of all trades. He'd take on a job fixing up an old house or sell items on online auction sites, or be part of multilevel marketing schemes. He did whatever it took to keep them afloat so they could live their dream in Theia.

Molly cradled her coffee closer to her chest. The warmth was comforting. "Okay. So you're working on something? Something more permanent, I assume. This sounds good, Dad. Why do you look like you're about to tell me something awful?"

"It's not awful. Not at all. It's great actually."

Something ominous was on the horizon. Molly could feel it in her bones. She put her mug down, not certain she wouldn't need her hands free in the next few minutes. "Okay. What is it?"

"It involves Persephone."

"Dad, if you tell me you are investing in the saloon, so help me—"

Jeb held out one hand. "No. No. Don't be so dramatic. I would never do that to you."

Her mother lifted an eyebrow. "It does involve Seph, and you really seem to dislike her, Molly."

"I do not dislike Seph."

Both her parents looked surprised at this revelation.

Her father leaned forward, his elbows planted on his thighs. "You don't?"

"No. Our battle over the saloon is not personal."

Her mother squinted at her as if she were staring at the sun. "It's not?"

"It's not. Can we move on. What is this business deal you've been discussing with Seph?"

"Do you remember the plan she outlined at the Primrose the other night about staying open year-round?"

"I remember."

"Do you remember her mentioning the bachelors' quarters?"

"Yeah. She said she could turn it into ten studio apartments."

"And what do you think of that plan?" Her dad bit his lip.

Molly shrugged. "I have no problem with it."

"Okay. Well, Seph and I were discussing being partners on the bachelors' quarters project."

Molly rubbed her palms over her thighs, the jean material sliding beneath her skin. She didn't like the idea of Seph pulling her father into her plans. But she hated that building, so it might be worth finding out exactly what Seph had in mind before making it another battleground. "Okay. So what does that mean?"

"Well, we're still hammering out details. And we haven't signed anything yet . . ." Jeb took a deep breath, expanding his chest. It was a signature move of his. He did it whenever he was about to drop something on his family like "I want to buy a new car," or "the Primrose needs new gutters," or "I think my computer got hacked."

Jeb waved his hand in the air. "The idea is that during the renovation phase, I would oversee the work, and Persephone would foot the bill. Then once it's up and running, your mother and I would oversee the management of the place while Seph's accountant handles the finances. We would split the profits down the middle."

Molly didn't have an inherent knack for business. But she'd had to acquire a head for it pretty quickly when she became self-employed. Her father was offering to input most of the labor while assuming none of the financial risk. "That seems fair."

"I thought so, too."

"Mom?"

Her mother snapped out of her mood in an instant. "Oh yeah."

Her father was much more enthusiastic. He clapped his hands together. "So? Do you both want to go down there with me tomorrow?"

Her mom was still making that face, so Molly jumped in to answer. "I'll go with you." She needed more information about this project, and it didn't hurt that it was something she could do with her parents.

Her dad reacted like a kid with a fresh ice cream cone. "You will?"

Janet finally snapped out of her pensive mood. "You know what? I think I will let the two of you go on your own."

Jeb turned to look at her, his brow furrowed.

She patted his arm. "It'll be a project the two of you can take on together if you decide to."

The furrow instantly melted, and he smiled at her. Molly had to admit to herself that she liked the sound of that, too.

"I have a meeting with Katie in the morning, Dad. So I can't go until the afternoon."

"No problem. Text me when you're ready."

Katie folded her hands together and placed them on top of the table. She shoved at her salad plate, moving it to give her room to lean over, her red hair curtaining over her shoulder.

"Here's the thing."

Molly put down her fork. She was nearly done with the salad anyway. And she wanted to save room for the club sandwich she'd ordered. "Uh oh."

Katie shook her hand. "Writers are so paranoid."

"We are."

"I know you haven't figured out a theme for the fourth book, and I'm not trying to pressure you to hurry up and figure it out."

Molly raised an eyebrow. "You're not? I thought that was a publisher's job."

"Look, I'd love a new manuscript ASAP. But that's not what I need to say to you right now."

Molly's gut flipped. If this meeting wasn't about her languishing manuscript, what could it be? The small indie publisher was going to drop her altogether? She wrote very specific books. Only so many options were open to her. She could self-publish. That was certainly a possibility, and she didn't mind that idea. She'd almost done that with the first book. What had stopped her was the result of her trauma over the magazine. Kelsy's stupid voice echoing in her head, telling her she'd never make it in the publishing world—that's what had held her back. All that fear bubbled up in her chest again as she waited for Katie to drop whatever bomb she was holding.

Katie sat patiently as their server collected the salad plates and refilled their water glasses. Then she refolded her hands. "What we need is something different."

"Different? You mean like not Theia, or not ghost town, or what?"

"I mean still Theia, still ghost town, but a new angle." She straightened her spine. "What people like about the first book is that it activates their emotions. They are either on Bub's side or the sheriff's side. They have skin in the game. They are mad that Bub died or hurt that the sheriff was shunned. It's a visceral reaction. The second and third books rode on that, Molly. People bought them because they loved the first book. But they didn't love those books in the same way. We've got to get that feeling back."

Molly needed to get it back, too. She'd been feverish when she wrote Bub's story. But after that it had become a chore. The book was a huge success, at least in its obscure genre, and she had to replicate that.

"I don't know how to recapture what I had then."

"Tell me what gets you fired up these days." Katie waved her hand. "It doesn't have to have anything to do with the town or history or whatever. What gets you fired up?"

The smooth skin of Seph's inner thigh is what got her really worked up. But while that might make a good novel, it wasn't appropriate for the ghost town series of books. "I'm completely pissed someone bought and is fixing up the Warsaw. That's what has me fired up lately."

"I heard about that. You want to write about your fight for the Warsaw?"

Molly shrugged.

"And what if you lose? You might lose."

Molly sighed. She was tired of the negativity. It would be nice to have someone on her side for once. Katie was as good a candidate for an ally as anyone. She, too, was making money on Molly's career. She could at least show a little support.

Suddenly, Molly was desperate to change the subject. "I don't know. I'll think of something and get it done fast. What have you been up to lately?" Molly sipped at her water and hoped Katie would take the bait.

"Oh, yeah. I've been meaning to tell you."

"Tell me what?"

"I went to a Northwestern publisher's convention last month. It was not medium specific, so there were all kinds of publishers there. Anyway, I met Kelsy."

Molly's stomach dropped all the way to her toes. She could

feel her spine curving as she attempted to stay upright in her chair. "Oh yeah?"

"Yeah. We were introduced by Helena; remember her?"

Molly didn't know who the hell Helena was, but she didn't care right then. "Yeah. Sure."

"Helena introduced us and in the process said that I publish books about Montana, including the famous ghost town series. Kelsy got all excited then. And that was super sus, because no one is excited when I mention ghost towns. Anyway, she asked me if I knew you."

An involuntary groan escaped Molly.

"Molly." Katie reached across the table and placed a hand on Molly's wrist. "You know that what happened isn't your fault, right?"

No amount of time with a therapist was going to take that sentence from being probably true to absorbed as a fact of her life. But Molly knew better than to argue. "Yeah. Of course."

"I didn't tell you this to cause trauma."

"It's fine."

Katie shot her a reproachful look. "Anyway, she was as polite as a snake. The interesting part is that when she walked away, Helena told me that Kelsy was being sued by a former employee for sexual harassment. And I have to ask—"

"It's not me."

"Oh." Katie cocked her head. "Do you want to talk to a lawyer because—"

Molly held up her hand, stopping Katie mid-sentence. Molly had had this conversation with every loved one in her life. Her parents, Etta, even Evelyn who'd somehow heard that she slept with her boss while she was out in Seattle, had offered to help her find a lawyer. And Molly was glad that someone had sued Kelsy. She did think that Kelsy should be held accountable for the way she used people. When she first left, Molly didn't know she wasn't the only one, and she'd made the decision to walk away and not look back. She was going to focus on her future now. And that future was in Theia.

"Let's get back to talking about the book. Maybe we could brainstorm together." Molly pulled a tablet out of her backpack. "I have a list of ideas started. Let's go through them one by one."

Katie folded her arms over her chest and stared at Molly. Eventually she shrugged. "Fine. Let's hear what you got."

Chapter Thirteen

"Hey, Dad. You made it."

Her father's leather sandals crunched on the gravel as he walked toward her. "Sorry I'm late." He slung an arm around her waist when they met up near the old log building that stretched out in front of them like a long house. "Everything okay with Katie?"

Her father had been her biggest cheerleader when she first decided to write books about Theia. She'd included him in every step of obtaining the contract with Katie's publishing company. And he and her mother had thrown a party when her first book was released. They had literally invited the whole town.

She didn't want to talk to him about her career right now. She didn't have any good news. She felt disconnected from her writing and, lately, her father, too. That's why she was standing here in front of the bachelors' quarters, to try to gain something back.

The ugly thing looked a lot like a very old, decrepit motor inn, the kind you might find along Route 66. Only, instead of a pink stucco exterior with bars on the windows, it was covered with rotting wood and featured gaping square openings where thin glass had once been.

Its aesthetic was as unappealing as its original inhabitants had been—young, rowdy miners in town to make a buck, drink, and frequent Madam Green's brothel. One of the unkempt drunkards who had once lived in the bachelors' quarters was responsible for the arson of the brothel in 1904, an act that maimed three ladies of the night and nearly killed the madam. The man was never caught because his identity was shielded by the other unsavories who lived in this place.

So, yeah, not exactly a beacon of goodness and joy.

"Let's start at the common room." Her father steered her to the far end of the building. The only set of double doors stood here, opening up to a room three times the size of all the others. When the building was in operation, it was used as a gathering space for the men, though largely they only ate meals here. They spent most of their free time at the bar or the brothel.

Molly and her father walked along the edge of the building, close enough to touch the logs that made up the exterior if they wanted to. They seemed to cry out to her that they had been stolen from their ancient forest and used for nefarious purposes. Could she please come and rescue them?

When they reached the doors, her father extracted a long, thick knife from a sheath attached to his belt. "When I was here last with Kyle, the door stuck something awful. We had a hell of a time getting it open, and we debated leaving it open, but Kyle didn't want to. Anyway, this might take a little doing."

Molly stayed close, ready to help her dad wrench the door open after he ran his knife along the seam. But neither the knife nor her brawn was needed as Jeb was able to easily pull the door open.

"Huh." He looked back at her and re-sheathed his knife. "That was easy. After you."

Molly wasn't thrilled about plunging into the dark, dank building first, but she stepped through the doorway and flicked on the penlight she kept attached to her keychain. Even with the afternoon sun streaming through the window openings, there were dark corners, and the dirt floor was uneven.

"Here's the main room." Her father's voice came from behind her. "There would have been tables and chairs in here for eating and a fireplace there." He pointed to a crumbling brick hearth along the far wall. "And the cooking would have been done over there." In the corner was another brick opening and the remains of several cast iron pieces. "This would have also held the only sink for washing." He pointed to a porcelain basin that sat in pieces on the floor. "And I don't think there is anything left of the outhouse, but it would have been out that door." He gestured to a now naked opening between the fireplace that would have been used for warmth and the stove that would have been used for cooking.

Jeb moved toward the hallway that extended from the back of the room. "All the rooms were connected to this space from here. Oh, it's dark." Jeb pulled a penlight out of his pocket and plunged into the windowless hallway.

Molly followed her father, her small light held high so she could see as much as possible. "We should have brought proper flashlights, Dad."

"Yep. When I was here with Kyle, he had a great big one and I didn't realize how dark it is. Guess I learned my lesson. Okay. Here's the first room."

They turned to the left and moved into a space that was nothing more than a small square with a single window. There was absolutely nothing in it except for a few weeds growing at the corners and several large spider webs. "This is what a single room is like."

Molly moved her light over the space. She tried to calculate the square footage, but wasn't really coming up with anything. "How big?"

"Kyle and I measured. They aren't all the same, but the rooms are roughly 300 square feet."

"You want to make 300 square foot apartments and have people live in them?"

"First, your cabin is only 450."

"Yeah. I guess. But it seems so much bigger."

"Second, people in big cities, like the one you lived in all through college, live in this much space all the time."

Molly couldn't argue with that. A studio apartment in San Francisco was not much bigger than this. "Yeah, but we are most likely talking about bringing Montanans and Wyomingites here to live. They are used to much more space."

"Maybe, but it's all part of the ghost town experience. To live like they did."

"No, Dad. Nobody wants to live like people did a hundred years ago. Seriously. Nobody."

He put his hand on her arm. "I know this is hard to picture right now. But these are going to be so cool. We'll keep the rustic look but completely modernize everything."

"What about the plumbing?"

She hated to rain on her dad's parade, especially when he looked so happy and excited, but there were practicalities that had to be discussed. If he and Seph were going to renovate this space, rather than simply tear it down, they had to realize the limitations.

Jeb waved his hand toward the hallway. "Opposite the hallway, along the back of the building, where it is hidden from view, we'll build beautiful bathrooms. One for every unit."

"They have to cross the main hallway to get to the bathroom? That seems problematic, to say the least. And what about the big slope out back? A few years ago we were worried this entire building was going to fall down the hill until Kyle shored it up with those boulders. How are you going to build bathrooms there? You'd have to backfill it first."

"We're still working on the details. Just walk with me." Jeb ushered her out of that room and back into the dank hall. He moved more quickly now, taking them to the next room along the way. "This one is slightly bigger. Of the ten units, I think about half are this size.”

Molly couldn't tell the difference in size between this room and the last one. That could have been because this one was not empty. The remnants of a cot frame sat beneath the window. A smattering of broken wood pieces were gathered in a loose pile along another wall. A large trunk sat in the center of the room, its closed lid covered in a thick pile of dust.

“What's all this?”

“Most of the rooms have stuff in them.”

Molly walked over to the trunk and pointed to it. “Like this?”

Jeb rubbed his chin. “I have to admit, I think that's the only trunk I've seen. I know there's a few chairs and tables in a couple of other units.”

Molly thought her father was downplaying such a treasure unless, of course, he already knew it was empty. “Have you or Kyle ever opened it?”

Her father shrugged. “Not me. I don't know about Kyle.”

Molly crouched down in front of the trunk. The lid was latched. A disturbance in the dust around it indicated that someone had, in fact, tried to get in. She jostled it for good measure, but it didn't budge.

“Is it locked?”

“No. There's no lock on it. I think the latch is stuck. Can I use your knife?”

Her dad seemed to pick up on her curiosity. He pulled out the knife and handed it to her before squatting at one end of the trunk. He braced one hand on the lid and the other on the bottom. “Ready.”

Molly examined the latch. Although it was clearly rusted, it was a simple latch without too many contact areas. She jammed the knife in the largest slot. Her dad yanked. There was a grinding sound, but no motion. She shimmied the knife on the other side of the latch mechanism, and the trunk flew open under her father's pull.

The scent coming from inside was not unpleasant. The sturdy wood had sealed it well. With two pinpoints of light roaming over them, the contents seemed to defy time, lying there as if to say, *What took you so long?*

"Looks like a blanket," her father said, his light focused on the neatly folded pile of fabric in the center of the chest. "We should not touch that. It's probably delicate. I'll take the trunk to Evelyn and see if she knows what to do."

Molly flashed her own light to the left, and it stuck there as her brain processed what she was seeing.

Jeb was moving his light over the area to the right of the blanket. "Books, maybe ledgers. I bet these are interesting, Molly. Molly?"

Molly had reached into the trunk, unable to curb her need to examine closer what she'd found. Her fingers carefully cupped the paper as she extracted a pile of letters, bound together with a sturdy-looking string.

"What do you have there?"

"It's got to be at least twenty-five or thirty letters." Molly turned to her dad. "I'm taking these home."

Whatever was in her eyes, and she was pretty sure it reflected the fierce fire burning inside her, kept her father from arguing. Molly stared at her treasure. Something big was about to happen. She could feel it.

Molly heard the knock on her cabin door, but she had no desire to move from her position on the floor, the letters splayed around her. So she called out for whoever the visitor was to let themselves in.

Jeb Green stepped inside, his arrival bringing a slight breeze that ruffled some of the letters. "Hey, pumpkin. You've been holed up in here for two days. What's going on?"

"Tread lightly, Dad. I've got a lot going on here."

He slowly picked his way over to the chair. "I can see that. Have you read them all?"

"Oh yeah, of course. I'm just putting them in chronological order at the moment. In fact . . ." Molly reached behind her onto the couch and produced a pad of yellow sticky notes and a pen. Once her father was fully seated in the chair, his movements no longer a threat to her project, she tossed them to him.

Jeb stared at the sticky notes, his nose scrunched up. "You're not going to stick these to—"

"Of course not." Molly slapped the floor. She'd removed her area rug so that only dark wood greeted her palm. "I'm going to stick them to the floor."

"Oh, right. Okay. So what am I writing?"

Molly called out the dates of each letter to him, ranging from June of 1897 to July of 1899. He dutifully wrote them down, then crawled onto the floor with her. She directed traffic as they set up a makeshift timeline on the floor and then placed the letters in the appropriate spots along it.

In the end, the string ran from the far corner of her kitchen to the fireplace. They used acid-free modern paper to place the more delicate letters on so they weren't touching the floor, making the sticky note timeline look even more like a confused mash-up of old and new.

"So." Jeb looked over at Molly from across the line. "What's the story?"

Molly grinned at her father. She was dying to tell it for the first time. This would be a verbal outline of what she would later weave into a tale for her book. No doubt she'd be up all night writing. She could feel the energy flowing through her.

"Coffee, on the porch of course."

"Decaf."

"I know. Go on out there and make sure the chairs aren't too dusty. I'll be right there."

Jeb headed out the door while Molly popped into the kitchen to make one decaf and one leaded cup of coffee. She hummed to herself as she prepared the beans. This was a special moment, and sharing it with her father only increased the spark of magic.

Once they were settled on the porch, each with a steaming mug in their hands, the sun setting behind the big house and providing the perfect glow for storytelling, Molly began.

"The letters are between Bridget Pollock and Elise Dupont."

"Wait. Two women? But we found them in the bachelors' quarters."

"We sure did." Molly smirked. "Seems Theia's life as an LGBTQ haven isn't new."

"Wow. Okay. So one of these women was living in the bachelors' quarters? Because I have to say, that's a bigger shock than anything else."

"Yes, Elise was. She was living there as Henry."

"Wow. Do you think she was trans?"

"I don't know how she would have identified if she'd lived today. From what I can piece together, Elise started calling herself Henry when she was a teenager and got her first job as a ranch hand. But she only called herself that to the outside world so she could make money and live on her own. She used her birth name and gender with her loved ones. This is pretty well established in her letters with Bridget."

"And how does she know Bridget?"

"She worked for a neighbor of Bridget's family, and that's how they met."

"And fell in love. Please tell me they fell in love."

Molly laughed. "They sure did."

"Awesome. Where was the ranch?"

"In South Dakota. But here's the thing. Bridget's dad was a righteous bastard. And Bridget's choices were to either stay under his roof or get married to some asshole her dad had picked out for her. So Elise left to make her fortune as a miner so she could swoop Bridget out of her life, and they could go off to live together. The dream was to own property and have a ranch of their own."

"I hope this story doesn't make me cry."

Molly shot her father a sympathetic look. "Way too many of our stories are sad, aren't they?"

Jeb took a sip of his coffee, eyes on Molly.

She took the hint and continued with the story. "All the letters are from Bridget. So we don't know what Elise wrote to Bridget except for inference from Bridget's replies. The first letter, from June 1897, appears to be a response to Elise's first letter when she arrived. In it, Bridget references being worried about Elise living in the bachelors' quarters. She asks if she should call her Henry in the letters to be safe. Super interestingly, it seems that Elise's response, whatever it was, calmed her fears. She calls her Elise and openly talks to her like she's a woman in the rest of the letters. She also refers to Elise's friend Peter, and she's grateful to him for helping Elise keep her secret."

"This is pretty remarkable for the time."

"Oh, it's more remarkable than that. As the letters go on, it appears that quite a few people came to know that Elise was a woman, but continued to treat her like a man. Bridget even references the time the 'boys' took her to the brothel. She is amused by the story so I'm assuming it ended to Bridget's satisfaction."

"Bridget and Elise stayed together, in love?"

"They sure did. Most of the letters are those incredible 'longing for you' letters that people used to write. People don't do that anymore."

"What happened to them?"

"The last letter, in summer of 1899, ends with Bridget talking about how she can't wait to see Elise. She can't believe Elise made all the money she did in the mines, and she is excited to start their life together."

Jeb frowned. "But Elise's trunk is abandoned in the bachelors' quarters six years before the town dried up. That doesn't bode well for this story."

"Well, here's the thing. I talked to Evelyn about the trunk."

"Oh. That was a good idea. Did she know about it?"

"Yes. The trunk wasn't abandoned here in 1899. It was brought here in 1971."

"What?"

"Check this out. Stan was one of the only people who regularly came to Theia back then. He was working in Bozeman, and he came up here on the weekends in the summer to check up on the place. That's also the summer he started fixing up the house he lives in now."

"We owe a lot of Theia's survival to Stan," Jeb said.

"A hundred percent. Anyway, according to Stan, one weekend a group of five people showed up in a van. When he came upon them, these people were hauling this trunk out of the back of the van and into the bachelors' quarters. So, of course, he stops them and asks them what the hell they're doing. They say they're fulfilling their grandmother's dying wish. At this point in the story he tells me that to him none of them looked at all related. But he took them at their word. He asked them what the dying wish was. They say that their grandmother told them she wanted this trunk to be left right here in Theia, that this was where it belonged."

"And?"

Molly shrugged. "Unfortunately, that's it."

"And he left it there all this time?"

"Yeah. He said it wasn't his place to mess up someone's dying wish."

Jeb tapped his nose. "That does sound like Stan."

"So, while I don't know who these people that dropped off the trunk were, I'm going to find out. And Kyle delivered the trunk to Evelyn today. She and her friend, who's an archivist, are going to go through it and report back to me."

"Is that everything we know?"

"So far. But, Dad. These letters." Molly threw her head back. "They're amazing. So tender. So sweet. This is a real love story. It's all here."

Her father examined her. "And?"

"And I'm going to write my fourth book about them."

Her father dropped his hand on her knee, reclaiming her full attention. "That's great, sweetheart."

"Yeah. And I have you to thank for the inspiration."

"I'm glad to hear that because I actually came over here to ask you for a favor."

"Sure, Dad. What is it?"

"Come with me tomorrow to meet with Seph and this architect friend of hers?"

Molly might have declined the invite outright a few days ago. But the bachelors' quarters held new interest for her, as did the prospect of being part of a project with her dad. She could set aside her issues with Seph regarding the saloon for this very different venture. After all, she was doing that on the regular to have hot sex with Seph. So there was really only one answer to her dad's query. "I'll be there."

Chapter Fourteen

Molly was a naturally punctual person. It was a good trait to have as a tour guide. She definitely got it from her mother, not her father. Jeb was known to rush into council meetings just as the gavel was coming down or slide in the door of the Primrose barely in time to carry a tray of cookies for evening tea.

So it wasn't a surprise that Molly beat him to their meeting. But that she was standing outside the bachelors' quarters all alone for a good twenty minutes was a bit of a shock. Seph was a professional businesswoman, a successful one at that. She struck Molly as a person that, if not always early, was at least always on time.

She eyed the door to the building, which they'd left cracked open, and wondered if she shouldn't just explore on her own for a while. She wouldn't mind a little more time with the place before its transformation began.

She moved toward the door thinking she'd hear them all arrive even from the inside, when the sound of voices penetrated the quiet. She looked toward the restaurant, but it wasn't open yet for the day, and it stood in silence.

Molly recognized her father's voice as the group approached, then Seph's. She spotted them soon after. They were walking with a tall, thin man with a tangle of curls framing his face. All three walked in step, laughing and speaking quickly.

By the time they reached her, Molly's mood had seriously soured. She'd gone from a feeling of connection and peace at being close to Elise's temporary home to irritation that she was, once again, the odd one out.

"Molly!" Her father greeted her like he hadn't seen her in months. "We're sorry we're late. We were just finishing breakfast."

Ah, so, her father had hosted them all for breakfast and hadn't thought to invite her. She stopped herself from pointing out the slight, and instead stuck her hand out to the man standing beside Seph. "Hi, I'm Molly Green."

"Bryan Kimble. Nice to meet you, Molly. I feel like I already know you, I've heard so much."

Molly bit her tongue, literally. She managed not to wince too much as she nodded. They were eating breakfast and talking about her not twenty yards from where she lived. Sure, that was great.

"Hi, Molly."

Unable to completely ignore her, Molly turned to Seph. She stood in the midmorning light, hair pulled into a low ponytail that draped elegantly over one shoulder. It was warm, and her light cotton top expressed that. Its butter yellow color and fluttery fit also showed Molly the curves that lay beneath. She wore a pair of brown leggings that hugged her thighs and calves in a way that made Molly want to trace their shape with her fingers.

"Hi, Seph. You all ready?" She spun away from them and led the way to the main door of the building.

Behind her, Jeb turned into tour guide extraordinaire. She was more than happy to let him do it. She was not in any mood to resume her usual duties. Besides, this was her dad's project. She was here for support, even if it felt like her presence was completely superfluous.

Once they were inside, Molly and Seph both floated around the edges as Jeb and Bryan talked about the bones of the building and how to preserve its nature while turning it into something people would want to live in. They took measurements and talked over details.

Molly appreciated Bryan's approach. He sounded as though he was truly committed to the building, its history, and its purpose. They spent a lot of time in the main room, discussing its possible uses, lingered in the hallway talking over plumbing options, and practically set up shop in the first sleeping room.

"Do you want to at least pop into the other single rooms?" Jeb asked.

"Oh, yes." Despite what had turned into a multi-hour adventure in the dank building by the light of four flashlights, Bryan's enthusiasm hadn't waned.

Molly glanced at Seph. She'd rarely spoken, but a near constant smile was planted on her lips as she shadowed Bryan and Jeb. Molly herself had stayed a little farther away from the rest, hovering in the doorway at the first bedroom.

As they moved toward the room Molly now thought of as Elise's, she took the lead, plunging through the doorway and gliding over to the window. Positioning herself at the head of the bed frame, she turned around to stare out at the room, imagining the view Elise had from here. The sun shone in from the window and revealed a slice of the big, blue sky Montana was famous for. It would have been perfect to write letters to Bridget by.

Though, more likely, Elise wrote her letters by candlelight after a long day of work in the mines. Molly was lost in imagining her, bent over a small desk, pouring her heart and soul onto the page for her love.

"Molly?"

She jumped, and her knee hit the edge of the bed frame. "Ouch."

Somehow Seph had snuck up on her. She was inches away on her other side. "So sorry." Seph bent over and gingerly touched Molly's knee.

Molly went still. Seph touching her bare knee where it was exposed beneath her shorts was no small thing. Her body's reaction completely shifted in that moment. Even as it did, her gaze roamed the room. Her father and Bryan seemed to have moved on.

Molly let out a breath. They were alone, though not completely. She could still hear the men's voices coming from the next room over.

Seph stood and looked at Molly with concern. "Are you okay?"

Molly rubbed her knee, more to recover from Seph's touch than to check it for injury. "Yeah. Sorry. I was just . . ." she fluttered her hand in the air, "daydreaming."

"I heard you found a trunk in here." Seph's gaze landed on the rectangle-shaped, dust-free space in the center of the room.

"Yeah. Evelyn has it. We're real excited about what it might contain." Why she omitted the letters, Molly wasn't entirely sure. She only knew that she wasn't ready to share Elise and Bridget with Seph yet. "Anyway, we should catch up with Dad and Bryan."

"Actually, I told them we'd meet them at the Oasis for lunch. I wanted to stay back and take pictures. And you were sort of standing here looking like you were . . . busy thinking."

Molly laughed as she imagined what she must have looked like, a statue with short hair and knobby knees whose only movement was to chew on her lip as her eyes glazed over. "Yeah. Okay. Have we been here long enough for the restaurant to open?"

"We've been in here a long time. Anyway, you could catch up with them if you want."

"No, I'll stay and help you take pictures."

Seph's smile was radiant. "Yeah? Cool. I brought a light. Maybe you could hold it?" She pulled a small ring light out of her shoulder bag and held it out.

Molly took it. "Absolutely. Where should we start?"

"May as well start in here. We could do all the rooms going to the end, then double back to the main room. I want to get a few shots of each. It shouldn't take too long."

"Okay."

Seph took several pictures in Elise's room, including a particularly artistic one of the empty spot where the trunk had stood for over fifty years. Then they went down the hall, taking pictures in each of the rooms.

The last was the largest, and it held the most furniture, almost as if it had become the storage room for the building at some point. A lot of the objects had clearly migrated this way, down toward the back door, and landed here.

A large, rectangular table, planted directly in the center of the room, took up a good portion of the space. Along the walls were smaller tables. A few were short and round, others tall and square. A dresser nearly blocked out all the light coming from the window.

Seph made her way into the far corner and beckoned Molly over. "Can you stand behind me and hold the light up over my head?"

They had done this in a previous room where a tree outside the window provided too much sun obstruction, so Molly understood what Seph wanted. She wove her way around the big table and shuffled into the corner. She and Seph were now jammed between the big table and a set of three small tables taking up the corner behind them.

Molly held the light high over Seph's head. Seph leaned forward, bringing her ass in direct contact with Molly's torso. If Seph weren't taller than her, Molly would be in an even greater struggle with her libido. As it was, she was hanging onto reason by a thread.

Seph was so close, her scent overwhelmed the stuffy room and penetrated Molly's brain, leaving it a fuzzy ball of mush.

Molly couldn't place the fragrance, but it was somewhere between flowery, clean, and pure sex.

Seph's long, thick locks, now freed from her ponytail, splayed across her back, moving the thin fabric of her blouse across her skin as it went. Seph stood and spun around, sending one swath of hair to whirl across Molly's neck.

They were pressed together. Seph still clutched the phone in her hand. Molly held the light above them both, its angle now shifted to cast Seph in a spotlight. As much as Molly enjoyed the view she needed that hand.

Molly flicked off the light and set it on one of the tables behind her. She took Seph's phone from her hand and did the same. Then she wrapped her arms around Seph's waist and pulled her in.

Seph gripped the back of Molly's hair, twisting it in her fingers as their mouths slammed together. The kisses were frantic, desperate even. There was no time to waste. They had to be touching, suckling, moaning. Right. Now.

Molly's hand slid down over the curve of Seph's ass and further still to her thigh. She paused for a fraction of a moment. The brown leggings put a damper in her plans. She had to recalibrate.

It wasn't easy to think with Seph's soft mouth on hers. But her desire led to ingenuity. She pulled away from Seph, gripped her own shirt with one hand, and yanked it over her head.

Seph's sly smile was accompanied by a pleased "Oh."

"It's not what you think." Standing there in her sports bra, Molly leaned around Seph, who took advantage of the movement to caress Molly's breasts with her greedy hands.

Molly threw her shirt over the big table at Seph's back, then gripped her waist. She gave Seph a saucy wink before spinning her around and bending her over the table.

"Oh!"

Molly's hands gripped the top of the soft, cotton leggings

and paused there. "You want me to stop?"

Seph folded her arms on top of Molly's shirt and rested her cheek on them. "Don't you dare."

Molly pulled the leggings to Seph's knees, dragging pink, lacy panties along with them. She ran her palm over both of Seph's ass cheeks before dropping them down to Seph's knees. She smoothed both hands slowly up Seph's thighs, her fingers massaging on their way.

Seph's breathing was loud and ragged as it echoed through the furniture-packed room. Molly tried to stay patient and steady despite the way that sound ramped up her desire. It was dim in the room without a light, but a sliver of sunshine eked its way through the window. It was enough for Molly to see the way Seph shivered when her finger slipped against her clit.

She moved her right hand with slow measured strokes while her left crept back up to Seph's incredible ass. Seph's forehead was pressed against her arm, and she whimpered quietly into Molly's T-shirt. Molly knew she was lost in sensation, not paying attention to anything other than the trail of Molly's right index finger.

And that's when she brought her left palm down on Seph's ass cheek. Seph's head popped up off her arm, and she emitted a low moan that was so sexy Molly thought her own knees might buckle in that moment.

"More?"

"Yes." Seph dropped her head back on her arm and huffed out a breath so hard dust scattered at the other end of the table. Molly's left hand gripped Seph's butt cheek as the fingers on her right plunged into her.

Seph let out a loud "Aaahhh" that sent shivers all the way through Molly's body, and she made her own sound. Seph looked back at her, eyes sparkling. She pushed her ass back onto Molly's hand. Molly temporarily released Seph's ass and used that hand to shove her shorts down. Then with cotton underwear to smooth skin, she slid Seph's thigh between her own.

Molly could feel the way Seph's hamstrings bunched beneath her as Seph indicated her approval of this new position. "Yes!"

Molly got lost in sensation, her own and Seph's mashed together in a flurry of motion, sound, and something indefinable that filled the air around them in a way that was as all-consuming as the dust covering its precious items.

The cries eventually turned to soft shivers and heaving recovery breaths. Molly kissed Seph's spine and helped her stand. She spun her around and planted a soft, sweet kiss on her lips. Seph stood there, looking a little dazed as Molly pulled up Seph's pants and brushed off the dust before pulling up her own shorts and retrieving her shirt.

One side of the shirt was coated in dust, having been the barrier between Seph and the table. She attempted to shake the shirt out, but the space was too enclosed, so she threw it back on and grabbed the phone and light before taking Seph's hand and pulling her through the furniture maze toward the hallway.

"You wanna finish taking pictures?"

Seph shook her head. "I wanna cuddle naked in a bed with you."

Molly laughed. "Not super practical at the moment. My dad and your friend are waiting for us."

Seph grinned and looked Molly up and down. "I think we're going to look suspicious."

Molly shrugged. "We'll say I had to crawl over some stuff to get you a good picture."

"Hmmm."

Molly leaned toward Seph. "Truth is I'm hungry now."

Seph dropped her head on Molly's shoulder and giggled. "Okay. Let's go."

Chapter Fifteen

Molly's dad slid over in the booth as she and Seph approached. "Hey, did you get good pictures?"

Molly plopped down beside him with her best poker face firmly in place. "Yes, I think so."

Her dad's gaze dropped to her dusty shirt. "Looks like you had some trouble."

Seph scooted into the seat beside Bryan and opposite Molly. "Yeah. There was a lot of stuff in that last room. We had trouble navigating it." She held Molly's gaze, her own neutral expression impressive.

Bryan plucked a breadstick out of the red plastic basket in the center of the table. "While you were gone, we have had so many ideas."

Seph flashed him an indulgent smile. "I bet you have."

"This entire place . . .," Bryan gestured outward with his hands, "is so incredible. And there are so many things that we could do here. I mean, you all . . .," he gestured to Jeb, "have already proved that with your renovated homes, and this restaurant, and the town hall."

When Bryan and Seph first arrived with her father, a bosom trio, Molly had felt she was on the outside. But somewhere between the incredible sex with Seph and Bryan's relatable enthusiasm, things had changed. She was still cautious about all the plans, especially given that Seph owned so many buildings, but the idea that she would turn Theia into Kekker had waned. Right or wrong, Molly felt she knew Seph enough to believe that.

Molly smiled at Bryan. "You've got the fever."

His dark eyes practically glowed. "You're right, I do. I might have to pick an old house to renovate and move into myself."

"Wait until you're done with mine, please," Seph said.

"So many cool places to live here. Speaking of which." Bryan clapped his hands together. "Let's talk about the bachelors' quarters."

Molly picked up the menu in front of her. "I want to hear everything. But I need food."

"Got you covered," her father said. "We ordered a bunch of stuff. Figured you both could eat whatever looked good. It should be here soon. Here." He slid a glass in front of her. "Etta said this was the perfect midday celebration drink."

Molly kissed her dad on the cheek. "My god, you're amazing."

"Agreed," Seph said. "Is this one for me?" She reached out and grabbed the drink that sat beside the breadsticks.

"Yep. Bryan said you'd like it."

Seph took a sip, and as she did she shot a look at Molly over the rim of her glass. Damn she was hot.

"Hmmm." Seph, her gaze still holding Molly's, licked her lips.

Molly mouthed. "Evil."

Seph turned away from her. "Ideas, guys, shoot."

Bryan turned over his paper placemat. "I need a pencil."

Jeb reached into his front shirt pocket where he *always* kept a blue ink pen, and pulled it out. "Will this work?"

Bryan eyed the pen warily but took it. He bent over the placemat with its scalloped edges while the rest of them waited. Molly was fascinated by his level of concentration as he drew, his brow knitted, tongue sticking out on one side of his mouth.

But her observation of his nearly comical focus was disrupted when Seph's bare foot landed on her calf. Instinctively, Molly turned to look at Seph. But Seph's head was turned away as she peered over Bryan's shoulder. Her toes, on the other hand, freed from her sandals, were walking deftly up Molly's leg.

Her foot stopped at Molly's knee where it came in contact with the bottom of her shorts. Then Seph pressed her arch against Molly's calf and dragged it slowly back down to her ankle again.

Bryan leaned back and pushed the placemat to the center of the table. "We don't want to add too much to the original building. We were talking about each apartment keeping its footprint, outside walls, and original window. But to increase the natural light, we could add small secondary windows in each room above the original ones." He tapped the paper. "They would be small and discreet, but I think they would really add to the ambience of the indoor space."

"I agree that more light is needed." Seph turned to Molly. "What do you think, Molly? Is it too much to add a window?"

Molly hadn't expected Seph to ask her opinion, but she was happy to give it. She leaned over the placemat. "It looks good on paper."

Seph tapped her chin with her finger. At the same time she tapped her big toe on Molly's ankle just above the top of her shoe. "Is there a way we could see what it looks like before we cut into the exterior wall of one of the rooms? It would suck to do that kind of destruction and then find out we hate it."

"Absolutely. I'll make a computer mock-up. Also, the way this construction is going to have to go down is that we'll have to remove the original logs and then remount them. So even if we did make a window and disliked it, we could put it back."

Jeb leaned forward. "And you'd barely know it was there. Molly, think of the Tolles cabin. We had to cut into the outside logs on the lower left side when that dog got stuck in there. But

Kyle and I managed to put the logs back in the same place and you can barely tell."

"I remember that," Molly said.

Seph's brow furrowed. "What happened to the dog?"

"He's fine," Jeb said. "He was a big basset, and he crawled in there, and we couldn't get to him. There was too much debris in the interior. We tried to move it, but every time we moved something, he freaked out and crawled deeper in. Finally, we decided the safest thing to do was to make him an escape route."

"A doggy door." Molly grinned.

"And he came out all right?"

Extreme got added to the words *dog lover* on the list of things Molly was learning about Seph.

"Yep," Jeb said. "He was fine. His person was visiting from out of state, and after a visit to the vet in Bozeman they went home happy and healthy."

"That guy sends a check to support historical preservation every year, you know," Molly said.

"The point is," Jeb said, "it can be undone if need be."

"Okay." Seph laid her hand on the table casually, while under the table, her foot began its ascent again. "What about the hallway? Does that stay how it is?"

Bryan bit his lip. "That's a bit of a problem. Because we absolutely can't add anything to the front of the building. It would ruin the historic look. We've got to preserve the façade. But we still have to add bathrooms, and preferably some closets in there somewhere too. If we keep the hallway as is, we would have to put each unit's bathroom on the other side of the hall. And that presents multiple problems, one of which is that that side of the building slopes away, so we'd have to build it up first, then add the units. You still have to leave your apartment to pee."

"Yeah. Dad and I were talking about this dilemma." Molly turned to look at Seph, who was giving Molly her full attention now.

Seph reached across the table, her middle finger touching the edge of Molly's palm. "What about . . .?"

The food arrived at that moment, tearing apart their tiny touch. The placemat got stored away somewhere as the server filled the table. Unfortunately, the shift also stole the contact of Seph's foot from Molly's leg.

After they each had a few bites to eat, Molly brought the conversation full circle. "What were you saying before, Seph, about the hallway?"

"What if we went down?"

Molly stopped in mid-motion, her hamburger hovering near her mouth. "Wait. What do you mean, exactly?"

"What if each unit had a basement beneath it that held the bathroom and bedroom, and upstairs in the original part of the building is the main living space. And we use the slope. We make the basement wall prop up the main building from underneath so that from the front you don't see the basement at all. That side will be completely underground. In the back, you would see a two-story building. On the bottom floor you could have windows and a door in the back for each unit. That gives each unit two entry points, one from the outside in the back that goes directly into the bedroom, and one from the main hallway in the original part of the building that goes into the upstairs living space."

Silence blanketed their table, allowing the noise from the now busy restaurant in full lunch rush to penetrate their little bubble. Molly broke the quiet by saying exactly what she meant in that moment. "That is freaking brilliant!"

"Yes," Jeb said. "You've doubled the living space, allowed for plumbing, and kept the historical character of the original building, all with one amazing idea."

Seph's smile was so proud and sweet it nearly blew Molly away. "Thank you."

"It's awesome," Bryan said. "I'll work something up."

They moved away from the subject of the bachelors' quarters after that. They ate and talked casually about their lives. Jeb discussed the new recipe Molly's mother had tried last night, which led to a discussion about favorite foods. Molly stayed quiet and absorbed new information. She discovered that Seph was a vegetarian but had struggled to make it work in Montana. She found out that, despite Kara's assertions about Seph being anti-kids, Seph did really enjoy being an aunt, and that her dog, Belle, was absolutely not into it and thought kids were the pits.

Molly also learned that Seph, very literally, could turn her on with the flick of her big toe.

After Seph and Bryan headed back to Bozeman for a family gathering at Kara's house, Molly and her dad walked back to the Primrose, enjoying the beauty of an early summer day. They stopped to watch a doe and her fawn grazing on the edge of a grove of trees. Jeb hooked his arm behind Molly's lower back, and Molly leaned into her father.

The deer startled, as did Molly, when her phone chirped with an incoming text.

"Who is it?" Jeb asked.

"Evelyn. I gotta go. She found something in the chest." Molly turned to walk in the opposite direction of the Primrose.

Her father kept up with her. "I'm coming, too." He rubbed his hands together. "I can't wait to find out what they have."

Molly shared that sentiment, and she picked up the pace as they strode down the long dirt road that led to Evelyn's place. After what seemed like an eternity, they arrived, slightly out of breath and a little sweaty, on Evelyn's doorstep. Within seconds of Molly's knock at the door, Evelyn threw it open and invited them in.

Evelyn ushered them into her cozy living room and settled

them on the couch opposite a severe-looking woman about Evelyn's age with a pair of wire-rimmed glasses and a bun so tight Molly worried that her brain might hurt.

"This is Harriet, my friend I was telling you about. She used to be an archivist for the state."

Jeb and Molly both stood and shook Harriet's hand before settling back down on the couch. "I'm sorry we haven't met before," Jeb said.

"I don't find ghost towns very interesting," Harriet said.

Molly wondered if she was making the same face her father was in that moment. "Really?"

"Aside from the occasional newspaper stuck to the walls, they don't generally have objects or documents of value. This trunk, however, is fairly spectacular."

"Should we discuss who really owns the trunk?" Jeb asked. "I mean, is the state involved or something? I don't want us to get in trouble here if we're messing with someone else's property."

Evelyn sat on the love seat beside Harriet. "Kyle owns the property the trunk was found on, and therefore he owns the trunk. However, since the sale is underway, I suppose Persephone is now the trunk's owner. And if you're her partner, yours too."

Molly clapped her hands together. "Great! So, what did you find?"

Harriet peered at Molly from over the top of her glasses. "Everything in the trunk appears to be from the late nineteenth century. We didn't find anything that would speak to its 1971 reappearance here in Theia."

"Okay," Molly said. "So whoever brought the trunk back here didn't mess with it between the time it was here originally and when they returned it."

"It would appear that way," Harriet said. "However, that's not to say they didn't go into it and look at the contents. They didn't add anything to it."

Molly didn't want to be impolite. And every bit of information was important, but she really, really wanted to get down to brass tacks. "So what's in it?"

Evelyn leaned back into the flower-print cushions of the love seat. "I think you're going to be very pleased."

Molly's knee bounced up and down. The suspense was going to kill her.

Evelyn and Harriet exchanged a glance. "Let's start with the blanket," Evelyn said.

Harriet got up and moved behind the couch Molly and Jeb were sitting on. There was a table set up in the corner, and Molly realized the trunk sat on top of the table. She couldn't see inside it from her vantage point, but she watched as the blanket emerged from the trunk, cradled in Harriet's careful hands.

"I have a lot of friends on the Northern Cheyenne reservation." Harriet carried the blanket back to her spot on the love seat. She sat gingerly and propped it on her knees. "I've worked with them on a lot of projects. And I'm certain that this blanket is of Cheyenne origin." She smoothed the blanket with her hand. "But I have an inquiry in to be sure. We sent pictures, and we'll know soon enough."

"That tracks with it being Elise's," Molly said.

"That's the letter writer?" Evelyn asked.

"The letter receiver, technically," Molly said. "All the letters I have were from her girlfriend, Bridget. And in one of the letters, Bridget alludes to Elise having spent time with the Cheyenne. Why or how, I'm not sure. She did speak fluent French, though, so maybe she was trading with the Cheyenne?"

Harriet held one hand in the air. "I'll find out."

Jeb slapped his knees, bringing their attention to him. "So, what else was in there?"

"Oh yes," Evelyn said. "The books. There were ledgers, as we mentioned. They were very interesting. This Elise, if she's the one who kept them, was extremely meticulous."

Harriet spoke up. "I'm almost positive that she's the one who wrote them. The handwriting matches the journal."

Molly's entire body buzzed. "Journal?"

Evelyn reached to her right. Beside her sat a small end table. A large green and brown lamp occupied most of its surface. She opened a drawer and pulled out a leatherbound book. "We know it was Elise's because she wrote her name on the first page along with the date she started writing in it in June 1897."

"Which corresponds to when she would have first arrived in Theia according to dates you gave me from the letters," Harriet said. "In fact, I suspect she bought it on the way here, perhaps from a trading post. I'm looking into which one."

Molly's fingers wiggled. "May I?"

Evelyn reached across the span between them and placed the journal in Molly's waiting hands. "This journal seems to go a little longer than her time in Theia. I think the last entry is about two months after the last letter. And it indicates that it was written in Colorado." Evelyn quirked up her brow.

Molly couldn't rip her gaze away from the journal. It sat in her hands like a magic ball that held all the wonders she could possibly imagine. Waiting to get home to crack it open might kill her.

Harriet gave her a few tips for reading it without damaging the pages. She wrapped it in a paper cover and tucked it carefully into a cloth bag before allowing Molly to leave with the treasure.

When they reached the Primrose, Molly said goodbye to her father and ducked into her cabin to be alone with Elise's thoughts.

Chapter Sixteen

Molly hit the enter button on her laptop. She had no choice but to finish out the already scheduled tours she had coming up. But she'd ensured that no new tours could be booked for the rest of the season.

She needed to spend as much time as possible investigating Elise, and until she saw the result of Seph's renovations, she felt like her tours were up in the air. Right now, her time was better spent on this.

She turned her attention back to the journal. Her approach to it was different than it had been for the letters. With those, she'd read them quickly and voraciously, going back to slowly wade through every detail and research each new piece.

With the journal, she was sorting through it line by line, carefully analyzing the meaning of every word. Each time she came across a new detail, she would jot it down in her lined notebook. In a few cases, she stopped to research dates and events before she moved on to the next entry.

She was still waiting for a lot of information. She perused the list on the first page of her spiral-bound notebook, its green lining and machine-punched holes a juxtaposition to Elise's old, leather-bound journal with its crisp, cream-colored pages. Gwen was working on finding any record of Elise or Bridget following August 1899. She promised to have a report by the end of the week, and Harriet was waiting to hear from her contact on the Northern Cheyenne reservation.

Molly set the notebook on her coffee table, picked up the journal, and leaned back in her couch. There were only a few pages left. She could feel the excitement building in Elise with every new entry.

Bridget had planned her escape. The last letter Molly had did not mention the plans. But there must have been some missing communication from Bridget, a telegraph perhaps, or even a letter from someone else that hadn't been included in the pile of saved treasures. Either way, Elise's journal entries made it clear that she was privy to what was about to happen.

Bridget's situation at home had become unbearable. It pained Elise every day to think of her love under the control of her unbending father. Elise had made enough money between her work in the mines and her work as an accountant for the other miners to set them up for a life together far away from Bridget's father.

Molly had painstakingly reread the letter where Bridget told Elise not to come get her. It was clearly a response to Elise saying she was going to be on her way back to South Dakota. Bridget sounded desperate when she begged Elise not to come. "He knows. He knows, and I fear for your safety. Please let me find another way. A way that will keep you safe."

The journal complemented the letters in terms of information. They were two pieces of a single puzzle that was their love story. But the journal was more than that to Molly because it was Elise's voice. Even when she was reading Bridget's letters, Molly felt a connection to Elise. There was a string bridging time that ran from Elise to Molly. She could feel it in her chest. And every word Elise wrote in her own hand seemed to speak directly to her.

Molly plunged back into those words she was so desperate to read. It seemed that Bridget had enlisted a neighbor to help her escape her father's farm. The stakes were high. Her father had plans to marry Bridget off to a widower a few towns over. Time was tight. The neighbor boy, Clint, was a good kid. He'd always been kind to Bridget. Elise wrote in her journal that she worried he secretly wanted Bridget for himself. She also doubted herself, saying that he was a good man who she'd worked alongside on the ranch. She admitted to herself in her journal that jealousy was the issue, not any real evidence of nefarious intentions from Clint.

Elise seemed to talk herself out of suspicion and into trust for Clint. A large part of that was because Bridget trusted him completely. In whatever communication she'd sent to Elise, she had conveyed that Clint was going to bring her to Theia.

So began what Molly called the "waiting game." Elise wrote a series of entries in her journal filled with worry. She had had no word, no way of knowing if Bridget was okay, only a yawning gap of time where she must wait. It reminded Molly of the movie about Apollo 13. The whole world had had no choice but to wait while the astronauts were on the dark side of the moon, not knowing if they would be okay when the crippled spaceship revolved around the lonely satellite.

The worry was tangible in Elise's writing, as were her feelings of helplessness. She considered herself Bridget's protector, and here she was with no way to save her from all the dangers of an 800-mile journey over land without the benefit of a combustion engine. Molly could feel the tension each day as Elise sat down after dinner to write in her journal.

Weeks after the last letter from Bridget, Elise was still waiting with no word. She wrote in her journal that she could barely breathe, she was so suffocated with anticipation. She wasn't mining anymore. She'd packed everything up, set up her finances, and was ready to move as soon as she had Bridget with her.

Her friend, Peter, had family in Colorado Springs. He'd written ahead and asked them to look for a piece of land Henry could purchase. He told his family Henry would be arriving with money from the mines and a new bride on his arm.

Everything was ready. She just needed Bridget.

Molly carefully turned the page. The date on the next entry was two weeks after the last one. She looked again to ensure she'd read it correctly. But there was no mistake. The longest stretch of time between entries was there, clear as the ink on the page.

This entry was different from the rest. Gone was the constant anxiety and fear. The tenor was joyful. It started with, "We made it!"

The passage was long and reflective. Elise wrote about her feelings alongside telling the story of Bridget's journey. While she was waiting anxiously in Theia and making arrangements for their relocation to Colorado, Bridget was sneaking away from the ranch in the dead of night.

She and Clint had traveled on horseback to the nearest train. Once in Montana, it took a while to secure a stagecoach ride. They had to act as husband and wife on every leg of their journey, and even then the Wild West reared its ugly head. Elise didn't go into detail, but both Bridget and Clint had struggles in keeping themselves safe.

They arrived in Theia and went to the inn. It was the innkeeper, Ryan O'Callaghan, who raised the alarm. He had received a telegram from Bridget's father. A description of Clint and Bridget had been sent to innkeepers in a number of towns throughout southeastern Montana saying that Clint had abducted the young Bridget and offering a reward to anyone who could safely return her to South Dakota. Elise stopped in the story to ponder how Bridget's father had discovered where she might be. Her speculation was that he had gotten hold of Elise's letters.

Elise picked the story back up with the innkeeper's warning. He suggested they leave town as soon as possible. He said that the bartender, Hugh Taft, had a soft spot for young lovers fleeing tyrannical fathers and sent them to the Warsaw.

Once there, Hugh hid Bridget in a small room in the back that he sometimes napped in or dropped overly drunk patrons in to sleep off their drink. Elise described the room as being a small rectangle, only long enough to fit a cot and wide enough to walk two paces between the door and the edge of the cot. It was small, and warm, and bare. And that's where Bridget waited.

Clint, meanwhile, went into the Warsaw to make quiet inquiries about Henry. He almost immediately ran into some of Henry's friends, and word got to Peter, who ran back to the bachelors' quarters to tell Elise her love had arrived.

Elise wrote about the feeling in her chest as she walked from her apartment to the bar. The way her heart beat so fast that she feared it would fall out. The way sweat beaded on her forehead and dropped into her eyes. She reached the Warsaw, and Hugh sent her into the little room.

And that's where the magic happened.

They were together again. They were touching, their skin sliding against one another, their lips pressed into a long awaited kiss. Elise wrote that the tiny room had been transformed from a drab prison to heaven itself.

Molly placed the journal carefully on the table. She wiped her brow with the back of her arm. Her own heart was pounding, her hands unsteady. The thrill of reading about Elise and Bridget's reunion had turned to panic.

She left her cabin, and in the same near-run as Elise all those years before made her way to the Warsaw.

"I need to talk to the architect, Bryan."

The man shrugged. "He's not here. We just follow his plans."

"Let me see them." Molly shook the metal fence with her

fingers. The gate lock clinked out a pattern that reflected her irritation.

The man on the other side of it eyed her. "I know you're the person trying to stop our project." He waved at the construction site behind him. "Why would I show you anything? Besides, it's not really my place."

"Well, whose place is it?"

"I mean, the lady herself is overseeing the work. I wouldn't do shit without her say-so."

"Fine. Let's get her here." Molly pulled out her phone and texted Seph. *Come to the Warsaw now.*

Molly stared at her phone. There was nothing. No reply. No moving dots. She looked back up at the man. He was backing away.

"Wait. Stop. You can't leave me here."

He pointed toward the gaping entrance of the Warsaw. "She's coming."

Seph emerged from the building. As she marched toward Molly, the man Molly'd been talking to backed away from the gate. "Thanks, Jack. I got this."

Annoyed at being referred to as "this," Molly was able to ignore the way Seph moved in a pair of tight jeans. "Seph."

"Molly. Hi." Even as she greeted her, Seph unlocked the gate and swung it open. "Good to see you."

"Hey, we have to talk."

"I gathered. Let's go inside." Seph walked toward the Warsaw, but instead of heading back through the front where the old swinging doors used to be, she walked around to the side of the building.

They passed the man Molly now knew was named Jack as well as three other men and two women, all involved in some carpentry project along the back of the building. Seph walked through another open door frame, this one the back entrance that Hugh Taft would have used to come and go from the bar.

It was also the entrance Madam Green and her ladies used so that any wives would not see them in the bar at the same time as the husbands.

And it was the door Clint and Bridget had slipped into with Hugh's help on that fateful day in 1899.

Molly followed Seph as she wove through the dark corridor behind the bar itself. This hallway led to the small office in the back, the door to the outhouse, and, if Molly was correct, the little room where Elise and Bridget had reunited.

Seph led her into the office. Molly wasn't sure what it had looked like back in Hugh's day. It had only ever been an empty room since she'd first laid eyes on the Warsaw, and there were no pictures she knew of that showed the office, unlike the few precious period images of the inside of the bar itself.

The walls were made of original old-growth logs harvested from the surrounding forest. They had a fresh coat of sealant, but were otherwise the same. The former empty space now held a small wooden desk and three spindle-backed chairs, one behind the desk and two in front of it. That and a couple of standing bodies was all there was room for. Molly had to admit that the decorations were tasteful in the space. Not that she'd ever tell Seph that.

Seph rounded the desk and picked up a roll of paper. She moved back around to the front and spread it out. Molly stepped up beside her to look at the architectural drawing. "You want to see what we're doing here?"

Molly wasn't sure how Seph had deduced exactly why Molly had practically run here in a full-on tizzy. But she did, in fact, know precisely what Molly wanted. The blueprints.

"We're not changing anything on the exterior, of course. We're restoring it, carefully."

Molly nodded. She believed that now, and she could see it in the work being performed behind the scaffolding. "What about inside?" Molly leaned over the table.

Seph copied her, placing her right hand directly beside Molly's left. With her free hand she traced the blueprint. "We're keeping the footprint of the main bar the same. We do have the roof collapse area on the east side. We're adding a support beam. Bryan figured out how to relocate it from what would have been the most obvious location, here." Seph tapped a spot on the blueprint. "To here." She hit another spot with her left hand while at the same time her right pinkie finger touched Molly's. "That way we don't obscure the view of here." Seph hit another spot, one Molly knew well, and turned to smile at her.

"Bub's poker table."

"Yeah. I have a guy reconstructing it from photos. I did search for the original, but as far as we can tell it was burned as firewood in the terrible winter of 1904."

"The last winter anyone spent in the original town."

Seph bumped her hip against Molly's. "Yep."

"Anything else?"

"Not in the main part of the bar."

"What about the back area?"

Seph returned her focus to the blueprints. "We're making a few minor changes to make it more functional. The bar will have more staff than it used to."

Seph seemed to wait for an acknowledgment, which Molly didn't give. She was warming up to the idea of the Warsaw being an operating business again, but that wasn't what was driving her now. Something far more important was at stake.

"So we're leaving this room as it is," Seph said. "Adding bathrooms here, and an access hallway here." Seph made motions over the blueprint.

"Wait." Molly honed in on the spot of greatest interest to her. "Where is the little room?"

"Little room?"

"Yeah." Molly stood and grabbed Seph's hand. She pulled her out of the office.

"Where are we going?"

"You have to see this." Molly dragged her down the hall. She found the door to the small space and threw it open, heaving a sigh of relief when she saw that it was still there.

The room was completely empty, four walls nearly on top of each other. It was smaller than Molly had even imagined. It was magical. It was special. It was important.

"Where is this room in your drawing?" Molly asked.

"We're tearing it out to make room for the bathrooms."

"You can't!" Molly's cry echoed through the room as if Elise and Bridget were there with her, adding their voices to her chorus of dissent.

"Molly, what's going on?"

"I'll show you." Molly picked up Seph's hand again and dragged her toward the front entrance of the saloon.

"Where are we going?"

"To my place. Now."

Chapter Seventeen

To her credit, Seph didn't argue. She kept up with Molly's frantic pace as they walked through town, marched down the dusty road, and plunged into the backyard of the Primrose and through the doors of the little cabin.

Molly sat Seph on her couch and went to retrieve the box she'd left on her kitchen table. The storage box was spacious, allowing both the pile of letters and the journal plenty of room inside. She hefted it by the built-in handles and carried the entire treasure chest into the living room.

"I have something I have to show you."

"Is this what you found inside the chest at the bachelors' quarters?"

Molly set the box on the coffee table and gaped at Seph. "You know I looked inside?"

"Evelyn told me."

"I didn't realize you were close with Evelyn."

"She comes by the site every few days to check on the progress of the renovations. So do Stan and Mayor Wright. You're welcome to come by anytime you'd like, Molly. I hope you know that."

Molly chose to ignore that statement. There was too much wrapped up in it. The town's acceptance of Seph. Her own unwillingness to participate in the process. She couldn't think about all that now. She had a mission.

Molly gestured to the box. "I have the letters and something else here, too. And I want to tell you all about it."

Seph sat back in the couch, a smile painted on her lips. "I'm all ears."

Molly sat beside Seph, angling herself on the couch with one leg up, her knee just barely touching Seph's thigh. Everything else fell away, and she told the tale of Bridget and Elise from the very beginning, weaving together every detail she had so far.

Molly could see Seph's interest grow with each new step in the story. By the time she reached the reunion in the little back room of the saloon, Seph was all in.

"And the date," Molly said. "Do you know what date Bridget and Elise's reunion was on?"

Seph shook her head. "No . . . wait . . . not?"

"Yeah. As far as I can tell, their reunion happened about six hours before the famous showdown on August 22."

"No way."

"Elise doesn't mention it in her journal. So I figure they must have been on their way out of town by the time it happened."

"That's crazy. Where did they go?"

"The last entry in the journal says they made it to Colorado Springs, and that this journal would be put away as they started a new chapter."

"So, what happened to them after that? And who were the people who dropped off the chest? And why did they leave it in an abandoned building?"

Molly laughed. "All great questions. None of which I have the answer to. Yet."

Seph placed her hand on Molly's lower arm. "How can I help?"

Molly tipped toward Seph, compelled to be closer to her. "There is something you can do." Even knowing that her request was a big one, and that this conversation could be doomed to morph into an argument, Molly's voice was soft and low. She couldn't help it. Being near Seph like this, breathing in her scent, anticipating her own lips pressed against Seph's, made it impossible not to be softer, more gentle.

"Oh my god!" Seph moved, startling Molly out of her sensual mood. "I can totally help."

"Yeah, you can." Molly was relieved she wouldn't have to point out the obvious herself. Seph would relinquish the point on her own and stop the demolition of the little room in the back of the saloon.

Seph pulled out her phone and started typing. Molly didn't try to see the screen. She merely sat back on the couch, content in the knowledge that Seph was texting her crew and telling them not to touch that precious little room. Or maybe she was telling Bryan he needed to redesign his plans.

Seph finished her text and shoved her phone back into her pocket. Then she turned to Molly and placed her hands on Molly's cheeks. "This is so exciting."

Molly licked her lips. Seph leaned in and kissed her.

What started as a celebratory kiss turned into something else. Not the unfettered passion of a kiss that started during a fight. This was softer, no less sensual, but certainly less urgent. Molly really enjoyed it.

But Seph pulled back, eyes bright. "I sent a text to an old friend of mine. Marcus Till. He's a genealogist who specializes in adoption and fostering records. If these people that Stan saw were the grandkids of Bridget or Elise, and they were the children of kids that they adopted or fostered, there might be a record of it."

"Even back then?"

"Yeah. He's found records that go all the way back to the orphan trains in the mid-1800s. He's incredible. He usually works for people with a deceased family member. All they know is that the person was adopted or fostered, and they know nothing else. Sometimes there isn't even a name of the fostering family if the child kept their original name. Still, he does it. He finds them. He's a miracle worker. So I told him I have a job for him in reverse. We know the name of the parents, and we want to know if there are kids. Oh, he's texting back."

Seph pulled the phone back out of her pocket and stared at it for a moment. "He's in. Says he wants to talk it through tonight. Can you send me all the details you have? Or better yet, let's call him together."

"I'm in."

Seph was as completely absorbed in Elise and Bridget's story as Molly was now. She would surely call off the demolition of the room. They'd solidify the deal after they talked to Marcus. For now, all Molly wanted was more kisses.

Marcus smiled back at Molly and Seph from the laptop screen. "This sounds like my kind of project."

"We're glad to hear it," Seph said. "Because it's very important to us."

Those words signaled that Seph was taking a stake in Elise and Bridget's lives. A part of Molly wanted to hate that. Bridget and Elise were hers. That sense of possession was what had kept her from telling Seph about the letters when they were touring the bachelors' quarters. But that had all changed. She didn't mind sharing them with Seph anymore. There was something about the four of them that felt like kin now.

"Is there any other information I could give you?" Molly asked Marcus.

She'd already downloaded every minute detail she had about both Elise and Bridget, much of it probably not relevant to his search through Colorado adoption records. But he didn't seem to mind. He diligently took notes on all of it.

"Any chance you could send me images of the letters?"

"I mean, sure," Molly said. "How would they help? They are between South Dakota and Montana, and before there were any kids."

Marcus cocked his head. He had an amazing set of long dreads, and when he did that, they slid down his shoulder. "Are we sure about that?"

Molly looked at Seph, who exchanged the same confused glance with her. Seph turned back to Marcus, tipping her own head. "Aren't we?"

"What about the last letter?"

Molly looked down at the pile of letters perched in her lap. She'd brought the entire box over to Seph's room at the Primrose to refer to during the conversation with Marcus. The empty box sat on the floor beside the antique chair she occupied. She held the letters, and Seph, seated on the edge of the bed, held the journal. Belle lay asleep in the center of the bed, very little help at all.

"What about the last letter?" Seph asked.

"Read me the last paragraph again," Marcus said.

Molly pulled out the letter and held it in front of her. "I can't wait to get the journey underway. The sooner I am in your arms, the sooner I will feel this weight off me. Though I suppose it won't actually go away; we will carry it together. I can't tell you how grateful I am that you are choosing me despite this addition to our party. I love you. I hope to be kissing you soon."

Seph swung her head back to Molly. "I thought she was talking about how she had to bring Clint with her."

"Why would Clint be a burden they would have to carry together?" Marcus asked. "Presumably, after he drops off Bridget he'll go back to his life. And even if he can't go back home because he helped her escape, he was a white man, so he could do whatever he wanted."

"Wait." Seph held one hand in the air. "Are you suggesting that Bridget was pregnant?"

"That is precisely what I'm suggesting. And if she had a baby—and keep in mind, we have no idea if she was coming with an actual baby in arms or one in the oven—in Montana or South Dakota, those letters and the places mentioned in them could help me track down the birth records."

Molly's head spun. "I don't understand. How could that be?"

Marcus frowned. "It was a different time. And there are, sadly, a lot of possibilities. One is that she was raped by an acquaintance or stranger, and another is that she needed to pay for Clint's services in an unseemly way."

"I don't think so," Seph said.

"Okay. Okay. But there is still sexual assault, and I'm wondering, you know . . ."

"No. What?" Molly asked.

"About her father."

"Oh man." Seph looked at Molly with a stricken expression.

Marcus continued down that dark path. "You have to wonder why her dad was so keen to get her back. He had to have spent a lot of time and money getting word out to every inn in every small town in southern Montana."

Molly set the letter back in her lap and smoothed it out with her hand. "He promised her to his friend. Maybe there was even money involved."

Marcus shook his head. "I doubt it. No, her dad wanted her back, and he had to have had a really good reason for searching so hard for a young woman."

"Okay." Seph walked over to where the laptop perched on the table. "Now that we're depressed, we'll get you those images and wait to hear what you find."

"Sorry, ladies. History is a bitch. But I'm all over this. And listen, if something as awful as I think happened to Bridget, that wasn't the end of the story. This much we already know."

"Thanks, Marcus. Talk soon." Seph turned off the call and snapped the laptop closed. She turned to Molly, handing her the journal. "Well, that was intense."

Molly placed the letters and the journal in the box beside her and rose. She and Seph were close now. She reached out a hand and placed it on Seph's upper arm. Seph dropped a hand on Molly's hip.

"Thank you for connecting with Marcus," Molly said. "It sounds like he could find something out. I'm feeling hopeful."

Seph placed a gentle kiss on Molly's lips. "Thank you for sharing Bridget and Elise with me."

Guilt swamped Molly over her original hesitation to tell Seph about the couple. There was no reason for it. Her possessiveness was childish and selfish. She had no greater right to the past than Seph did. And it seemed even more petty in light of how she now viewed herself and Seph as a team, warriors trying to protect Bridget and Elise and their legacy.

"So, can we talk about the room?" Molly asked.

"I'll talk to Bryan and see what we can do."

That wasn't the enthusiastic answer Molly wanted. "Meaning what, exactly?"

"It's not as simple as saying we'll change the construction plans."

Molly took a step back. Suddenly, being this close to Seph felt suffocating. "Yes, it is. It is that simple. It's your project. You're paying for it, so change the plans."

Seph sighed. Her hands, now freed from touching Molly, dropped to her sides. "I need that space to make everything work, Molly. I don't know if I can set it aside."

Heat rose through Molly's chest. "You have to."

"I'm not saying I won't. I'm saying, I need to take a look at it."

"You need to call your work crew right now and tell them to leave that room alone. Then call Bryan and tell him you're changing the plans. Get him down here tomorrow."

Seph crossed her arms over her chest and pursed her lips. "I'm not taking orders from you or anyone else. This is my project, and I will make the decisions."

Determination was written on Seph like a billboard screaming out at the passing traffic. Seph had never been so relatable to Molly. But she needed to make her understand that she, too, had her heart in this. "Seph, I get that this is your project, but this is bigger than you."

"Elise and Bridget matter to me, too. Didn't I just prove that?"

"It matters to me more because it's all I have."

Seph's face softened. "What do you mean?"

Molly felt the crack in her resolve getting larger, and she attempted to fight it. She heard the break in her voice. "I lost everything I had worked for at the magazine because my stupid ass slept with a rich woman in power. And when I asked her for more, she stole everything from me." She hit her chest. "Is that what you're going to do?"

Seph took a step forward. "No, Molly. I'm not. I'm so sorry that happened to you, but I'm not your boss. I'm not wielding any power over you."

"Yes, you are. You have control over the one thing that lifted me up after the magazine. I owe everything I have now to the Warsaw, and *you* control it. You are lording it over me. You want to see me break!"

"Molly, no, that's not true. Please. Sit down." Seph gestured to the bed. "Let's talk this through."

Molly knew there was no way she could have a conversation now. Her emotional floodgates had been opened and the water was pouring out with a devastating force. She picked up the box that contained the love story she'd become consumed with and backed toward the door. "Not now."

"Okay." Seph held her hands out. "Not now. But we will talk

about this, Molly. And we'll work it out."

Molly didn't respond. She yanked open the door with her free hand and rushed out.

Chapter Eighteen

The sky was clear, allowing billions of stars to light Molly's way. She readjusted the backpack on her shoulders as she walked past the Bothwood mansion which Seph had purchased as her future home. Like the saloon, it was in the process of renovations, but the work happening now was largely on the interior. And since it wasn't livable yet, it stood empty and quiet at five in the morning.

Molly stopped to stare up at the regal home. For its time and place, it stood out. Rich décor adorned the gabled roof. The broad wings on either side of the main part of the house swooped out, showing off its ample size. But it had always been the wide wraparound porch that intrigued Molly. It spoke of a time when the richness of a person's life could be measured in glasses of lemonade and sunsets.

It also reminded her of that night so many years ago that she and Seph spent on a much less regal porch staring out at the streets of Berkeley and getting to know one another. She could imagine them sitting on the Bothwood porch next summer, perhaps swinging, probably laughing, definitely kissing.

But she was about to put a wrench in all of that. So she tore her gaze away from the porch and turned onto Elm. She walked the length of the Bothwood property and headed toward the old hotel. In this part of town, there were no lights, not yet at least.

But Molly had no trouble finding her way in the dark. She knew her way through these buildings and over the rough ground like she knew the pathway from her cabin to the Primrose.

When she'd first moved back to Theia, this part of town, which had seemed sad and lonely during her childhood, had come to life for her. The more she dug into the stories of the past, the greater her attachment to each old board and rusty nail had become.

The place had to be preserved in some sense; otherwise, it would be lost to time forever. Molly knew that, even if Mayor Wright had questioned her understanding back at the town meeting. But she'd always hoped that this part of town, unlike the ring of homes and businesses surrounding it, would remain like it was now. Replacing rotting wood and shoring up foundations was a far cry from what Seph was doing with the Warsaw.

The mayor's argument was that Seph wasn't doing anything different than Janet and Jeb had done when they renovated the Primrose and turned it into a bed-and-breakfast, or what Kyle had done when he fixed up and turned the brothel into a restaurant and bar. That argument had landed with Molly. But that was the outer edges of town. Molly wanted *this* part of town to stay the same. And she thought others agreed with her. They were all in it together when they pursued historic designation.

Now her friends and family were behind Seph, and she had nearly been there, too. Until Elise and Bridget barged into her life, and preserving their history became Molly's new mission.

The Warsaw was quiet and still. Despite the ugly fence and horrible scaffolding, there was something peaceful about it in the predawn quiet.

At 5 a.m. in 1899, it would have been quiet, too. Hugh Taft would have been tucked into his one-room cabin which sat in the back part of the property. The little log building was gone now, lost to a fire sometime in the 1920s, which Stan's father and a handful of firefighters had managed to keep from spreading to the other buildings. In 1899, it would have been there. And while Hugh dreamed away, a drunk patron might have been sleeping in the little room with the cot at the back of the Warsaw. On the other side of town, the miners would be eating breakfast at the bachelors' quarters, preparing for a long day of work, and the brothel, which now housed the Oasis, would have been sluggish with sleep.

Molly broke the quiet with the clang of metal as she climbed the fence around the saloon. It wasn't nearly as hard as she'd imagined it might be when she first saw the behemoth. She did it with her pack still on her back and managed to acquire only one minor scrape. She looked back after having vanquished it. A sense of triumph flooded her though she didn't have time to revel in her victory over a metal foe. She turned toward the Warsaw and headed to her destiny.

Molly grinned. "Jack, right?"

The man nodded, his eyes so wide they looked like they might fall out of the sockets.

"I think you'd better call your boss."

Jack hadn't spoken since his original exclamation at finding Molly at the Warsaw. After his shout, he'd examined her setup. It was pretty brilliant. She'd wrapped a chain all the way around the large tool shed that sat in the far corner of the property. It was technically outside the bar itself. She'd watched the workers put all their necessary tools into that shed, and she knew they couldn't do a thing without it.

She'd looped a handcuff through the two ends of the chain and then stuck one hand inside, locking it all together. She sat on the ground in front of the shed's door and waited.

Two hours later, Jack arrived, at least six other people on his heels. He looked a bit like a cartoon character coming to an abrupt stop. Molly could almost hear the sound accompanying his feet planting themselves on the dirt a few yards away.

Jack did as he was told while the rest of the crew wandered around the yard behind the saloon sipping from thermoses and shooting one another looks, but not saying much of anything.

The uncomfortable atmosphere didn't bother Molly in the least. Never having done anything like this before, she hadn't been certain how she'd react to being discovered. Would she be able to hold onto her ire and carry out her plans in the face of resistance and possibly even ridicule?

She'd run through a few scenarios during her wait. They all involved some sort of yelling and hysterics. But this quiet confusion emanating from the crew bolstered her resolve. She liked this feeling. It mirrored the discomfort sitting in her chest over this entire situation.

Seph arrived within twenty minutes. She did not, as Molly imagined, march in with the fire of anger flaming around her. Instead, she looked weary. Her hair was gathered in a messy bun at the base of her neck. Her face, scrubbed of makeup, showed signs of fatigue. She wore leggings and one of Molly's hoodies that she'd kept after a particularly steamy encounter.

The first people she spoke to when she entered the yard were the workers. She thanked them all for showing up for the day and said they would get a late start. She suggested they head to the Primrose for coffee and tea. As the workers filed out, Seph bent over her phone to send a text.

When she was done, Seph shoved the phone in her hoodie pocket and looked at Molly. "What's this?"

"Isn't it obvious?"

Seph signed. "I told you I will talk to Bryan about the back room."

"I need a promise. A commitment."

Seph examined her. Her eyes roamed over Molly's face. "To the saloon or to you?"

Molly startled, her head flying back. "What?"

Seph dropped to the ground, sitting cross-legged opposite Molly. Her hands rested on her knees. "Because if you're looking for me to tell you that I want to be with you, I do, but it's complicated."

This was not at all the conversation Molly was expecting to have, and she had to recalibrate her brain. She stared at Seph for a long beat, trying to catch up. Did she want to be with Seph in a more substantial way? Probably, yeah. That wasn't her priority right now. Seph obviously felt the same way.

"Complicated because of this?" Molly held up her handcuffed hand.

"No. I think we can work through everything with the saloon. It's us that's complicated."

As much as Molly wanted to get back to the subject of the saloon, she was curious. It might not hurt to find out what Seph was thinking. "Complicated how?"

"My divorce is still fresh. I have a lot of baggage that I brought with me when I fled my life in California and came to hide out in Montana."

"What were you running from? I mean besides the ex-husband."

"I wasn't running from him or our joint friends and business partners. Though that's what everyone thinks. I can't tell you how many times a day I hear from people in my life back in California telling me that they will welcome me home with open arms. Even Greg himself has told me that we can work things out in terms of sharing friends and taking turns at social events. They all think I'm running away out of embarrassment or grief for my old life, or some such thing."

Molly completely understood what Seph was saying. She'd been greeted with similar reactions when she left Seattle. It wasn't an illogical assumption that she would hide out of embarrassment and shame. "But you're not running from that."

"No. I'm not running away at all. Not really. I'm looking for my own path. I need something that is mine, all mine. And I know." Seph held up her hand. "I know that you think I'm stealing what's yours. But I swear, that's not what I'm trying to do."

"Theia is my path, too."

"I know." Seph reached out her hand and placed it over Molly's free one. "And I think we can find a way to share it. And if we can do that . . ." She tipped her head and presented Molly with a soft smile. "Maybe we could find a way to be together as well."

"But we both have to unpack our baggage first."

"We do."

"This," Molly lifted her cuffed hand again, "is me unpacking my baggage."

Seph let out a heavy breath. "Could we maybe find another way to do it?"

"Nope. I need you to help me out with this, Seph."

"Bryan is in Florida with his husband and kids for a couple of days. I will text him, and we'll talk about it when he comes back."

"Good. In the meantime, you can make a promise. Write it down. That's all I want. A piece of paper, signed by you, saying you won't destroy the back room."

Seph ran a hand through her thick, silky hair. "I'm not making my decisions because it's what someone else wants anymore, Molly. I'm not signing away my rights to be in charge of my own projects anymore. I'm done with that. This is part of my journey."

Molly's mind flashed back to the conversation where Seph explained her engagement to Greg. The ultimatums. The heavy-handedness. Something dropped into the pit of her stomach. Did Seph see Molly as doing that to her now?

"I'm not trying to tell you what to do. I'm asking for your help."

Seph's eyes grew wide. "Really?" She lifted her hand off

Molly's and gestured to the chain. "So this is asking?"

"Yes, I'm asking. And if you won't do it, I'm going to continue to ask, in new and challenging ways. It's not me forcing you to do something. It's me continuing to advocate for what I believe in. So, will you make a commitment?"

"I can't."

"You *can*. You won't."

"This is me unpacking *my* baggage."

"Okay. Then call the sheriff."

"What?"

"Call the sheriff. His number is in my phone." She dug her phone out of her cargo pocket and handed it to Seph. The number was already pulled up.

The phone lay on Seph's palm as she stared at it. "No."

"I'm literally chained to your tool shed. I have stalled out your project. I trespassed on your property."

Seph grabbed Molly's free hand and shoved the phone back in it. "I'm not calling the sheriff."

Molly knew that with Seph this close she risked losing her nerve. She could feel herself backing down. "Fine. Then I will." She hit the button.

Seph dropped her head and rubbed her eyes. "Good lord."

"Sheriff's department."

"Hi. I have a trespassing issue here in Theia."

"Okay. I have to tell you it will take our deputies at least a half hour to get out to Theia, and trespassing is low on our list. Can you tell me more about what's going on there? Who is the person on your property?"

"A protester that's chained to a tool shed."

Seph shook her head.

"Okay. I see. And have they put themselves or others in danger?"

"No. But they stopped work at an active construction site."

"Okay. And have they damaged any property?"

Molly stared at the phone and looked up at Seph. "Yes, she has."

"No, she hasn't," Seph shouted at the phone.

The operator must have thought that Seph was the protestor. "That is serious. I will send my nearest deputy. Do you want to stay on the line with me? Do you feel safe?"

"I'm good. We'll see you when you get here." Molly quickly hung up the phone before Seph could say more.

"Seriously?"

"I did what I had to."

"Molly, can we talk this out? I will send the work crew home. We can go back to your place and talk. Or the bar, because honestly I haven't had my coffee yet, but I could use a drink of something stronger right now."

"It's not going to be that simple, Seph."

"I'm not pressing charges."

"You won't have to. Step back."

"What?"

Molly slipped her free hand into her backpack and pulled out a hammer. "Move back."

Seph jumped to her feet. "What are you doing?"

"Just a bit of damage. Enough to make sure the sheriff has no choice but to get involved. Then we'll involve a judge and the whole town. I'm tired of everyone overlooking this issue. This . . .," Molly hit the shed door with the claw side of the hammer, making a slight dent in the plywood, "will make it all very public."

Seph stood over Molly. She watched Molly take another swing at the door before turning on her heel and walking away.

Chapter Nineteen

Sheriff's Deputy Alex Klepper was the one to respond to Theia most of the time. Not that many incidents required her to come in the first place. There was the occasional drunk and belligerent tourist or kids from out of town throwing a party and shooting up a sign or spray-painting something they shouldn't. In general, it was a quiet place.

Wherever Alex had been when the call came in, it was taking awhile for her to arrive. Molly was alone during the wait. She had no idea where Seph had gone. And the workers never returned. It would have been quiet and peaceful out there under the big sky in the middle of the ghost town if her parents and Etta hadn't disturbed the calm with their constant calls.

She let the first few calls go to voicemail, not really in the mood to explain herself yet. Instead, she practiced her speeches. She expected to have many. She'd have to tell one story to the deputy, one to the justice of the peace, and of course there would undoubtedly be the council, the mayor, and a lot of other folks in town.

Her phone kept disturbing her, and she finally answered Etta's call. She figured Etta would be easiest. It turned out not so much.

"Seriously? What the hell are you doing?"

"Making a stand."

Etta let out a long-suffering sigh. "You are not a college student protesting a war. You are a thirty-something lesbian with career issues and a severe fear of commitment. This is not how you deal with any of this."

"I made my bed, and now I'm going to lie in it." Molly paused to listen to the background sounds on Etta's phone. "Where are you? The restaurant isn't even open yet."

"I'm outside the fence in front of the Warsaw."

"What? How did you even find out about this?"

"Everyone knows, Mol. And they're all here."

"What do you mean, here?"

"Half the town." Etta paused. "Hmm. Dale has arrived, too. Oh, and Clinton and her wife. Yeah. Maybe more than half the town. We're all out here, waiting to see what happens when the sheriff arrives."

"Is Seph out there?"

"No. Don't know where she went. But your parents are both here. Wanna talk to them?"

"God, no. Can you, like, get everyone to leave?"

"Sorry, Mol. That's not happening."

Molly couldn't see the fence from where she sat. The tool shed was tucked behind the Warsaw so Molly was hidden from the gathering crowd, and they from her. But as her wait stretched on, waves of conversation floated through the air to her ears. She couldn't make out any individual voices or what they were saying. She felt a bit like a zoo animal hiding in its makeshift cage, the sounds of the crowd outside the fence anxiously waiting for her to emerge and give them a show.

Eventually, the clinking of the gate opening created a hush among the crowd. Boots shuffled along the gravel and dirt. Deputy Klepper rounded the corner and came into view.

Molly greeted the deputy with a wide smile. "Hi, Alex."

The deputy stopped a few feet in front of Molly, hooked a thumb on her belt, and examined her. "What's going on here?"

"I'm standing up for what I believe in."

Alex removed her hat, scratched her head, and set it back down on her short, dark hair, not unlike Molly's own, but with shorter bangs. "Looks to me like you're sitting."

"I'm chained to the shed."

"I see that. Wanna tell me why?"

Molly gestured with her chin toward the fence. "Didn't they already tell you?"

"I wanna hear what you have to say."

"I'm trying to save the Warsaw from destruction."

"Hmm." Alex pivoted, suddenly walking away from Molly. She moved to the back door of the saloon, threw it open and walked in, leaving the door gaping open behind her.

Molly was tempted to follow, but that would mean unlocking herself. And even if she wanted to do that, she couldn't. She'd left the key back in her cabin, appropriately, she thought, tucked into the box holding Bridget's letters and Elise's journal.

Alex was inside for a few minutes. When she came back out, she sauntered to Molly's spot. "Have you been in there lately?"

"Yeah."

"Doesn't look destroyed to me. Looks like it's being lovingly restored."

Molly huffed. "That's a matter of opinion."

Alex raised one eyebrow. "Well, I'm not sure it's worth chaining yourself to something."

"It is to me."

"Okay, well, the owner doesn't want to press trespassing charges."

"I walked through federal property to get here. I passed that little piece that belongs to the forest service."

Alex sighed. "You know as well as I do that no one cares about that."

"What about the damage I did?" Molly scooted over to show the hole she'd managed to poke in the shed. "That's property damage in a place that is up for historic designation. That's gotta count for something."

Alex squatted down, her elbows on her knees, hands hanging down in front of her. "What's your end game here, Molly?"

"I want you to arrest me, and I want to go before JP Miller."

"You know he's two days into a weeklong fly fishing trip, right?"

Molly had not known that. It meant either waiting for his return or getting someone else from another part of Montana to come down to Theia for her hearing. "I'll wait."

"Okay." Alex rose. "I guess we can do that."

Three or four days in county lockup was not in Molly's plan, but she'd come too far now to go back. "Okay. So you're taking me to the Bozeman jail?"

Alex shook her head. Molly let out a breath. She'd at least be comfortable at home while she waited for her hearing. Then Alex explained. "I already talked to JP Miller. We decided to keep you here, in Theia. At the local jail."

"We don't have a local jail."

"Oh, you do."

Molly's brain whirred. Alex couldn't possibly mean the two-room jail at the back of the courthouse. The dank, drafty space was built at the same time as the courthouse in 1898, and was last used in 1905. When the courthouse was renovated and electricity and plumbing were installed, the jail was left untouched. There wasn't so much as a bare lightbulb hanging in the place.

Alex pulled a key from her pocket and knelt beside Molly. Molly recognized the key as hers at the same moment that Alex stuck it into the handcuff lock and turned. "Your father found it."

"Of course he did."

Once Alex had her unhooked from the chain, she helped Molly to her feet. "You're gonna come with me, right?" Alex held up Molly's handcuffs.

"Yeah, sure."

"Okay, here." Alex handed Molly the handcuffs. "Is that your bag?" She gestured to Molly's backpack.

"Yeah." Molly reached down and shoved the handcuffs back in her bag. She left the chain where it lay on the ground in a now broken circle around the shed.

"Bring your bag with you."

Molly hefted the bag onto her shoulder and followed Alex around the corner of the Warsaw. That's when the crowd came into view. It was as big as Etta had said. Her parents were there, of course, and Etta and Kyle. Evelyn was there with Stan. The mayor was there along with a handful of other people. All in all, it was about half the town. One person was conspicuously absent—Seph.

"I see news travels fast," Molly said. She had, of course, counted on that.

"Molly, what were you thinking?" her mother asked.

Alex held up her hand. "We'll talk about this later. I need to read Molly her rights and take her to the jail. Everyone back up." She waved her hand at the fence.

The crowd moved, allowing Alex to open the gate so she and Molly could slip through.

"What jail?" her dad asked.

Molly just laughed.

The room was slightly better than Molly had imagined. She'd actually never been in the jail space. The floor was not dirt, like so many of the cabins in the ghost town park. It had a wood-plank floor that appeared to Molly to be remnants of the flooring in the Warsaw. The short planks were pieced together to cover both the tiny entry area and the two small cells in the back of the space.

To make the jail secure, the builders had used brick instead of wood or logs for the walls. It kept the place slightly less drafty. The bars that separated the cells from each other and the lobby area were cold, hard iron.

That was it. There was no furniture, not even a chair. Molly stood in her cell and peered through the bars at Alex. "Are you seriously going to leave me in here for four days?"

"Yep." Alex clutched the key she'd used on the padlock she brought to close the cell. Then she hung it from a nail jammed into the mortar beside the door.

"No, wait. Alex!"

But Molly's calls went unanswered as Alex marched through the doorway, leaving the heavy wooden door open behind her.

Molly stared at the open door for what had to be nearly twenty minutes before her mother, closely followed by her father, burst through it. Her mother ran straight to the bars and gripped them with her hands as if she were the one locked behind them.

Molly squeezed her mom's hand before turning her attention back to the door. Bodies were still pouring through it. Mayor Wright, Etta, and Kyle all jammed into the tiny area between the door and the cells.

Everyone was talking at once, and Molly couldn't quite discern what any of them were saying. She was pretty sure someone said "not what we meant," which definitely caught her attention. Exactly who said it in the mish-mash of voices, she couldn't be sure.

Before Molly could catch any more tidbits out of the flow of conversation around her, Mayor Wright whistled. The loud, piercing sound stopped all others.

"Now that I have your attention," she said, "I would like everyone to please calm down." She shouldered through the bodies packed into the minuscule space until she was standing beside Janet Green. She blatantly examined Molly from head to toe. "You look all right."

"I'm okay. I mean, I could use a place to sit." Molly glanced back at the empty cell before turning back to the mayor. "But I'll survive."

The mayor bit her lip and glanced over at Janet.

"This won't do," Molly's mother said.

"Hang on." The mayor pulled her phone out and dialed a number. She held up her hand in a signal that everyone in the room seemed to automatically recognize as the need to stay quiet. After a few beats she spoke.

"Henry, hi. It's Margo . . . Yeah. Yeah. So I heard you aren't coming back for four days . . . right . . . so, the thing is, Deputy Klepper put Molly in the old jail . . . oh . . . I see . . . don't you think maybe . . . okay . . . okay . . . I won't . . . okay . . . see you when you get back to town." She put the phone back in her pocket.

"Well?" Jeb asked.

Mayor Wright turned so she was facing the crowd, her back to Molly. "He said it was his idea to put her in here, that he is not coming back early, and that no one is to disturb him again."

"This is nuts!" Janet was working up a head of steam, and Molly could see her moving toward a full meltdown. Her mother was usually a fairly chill person. She'd spent years handling classrooms of screaming kids in a calm, collected manor. But she was a mama bear through and through.

"Mom. Mom. It's okay," Molly said. "This is my doing."

Her mother whirled around, eyes bright.

"Really. It's not that big a deal, Mom. It's like camping out, right? Honestly, it's way better than county lockup."

"She's not wrong," Kyle said.

"This building is old and drafty," her mother argued.

Molly shrugged. "Good thing it's summer."

Her mother made a noise that emanated from deep in her throat.

Before Molly could figure out what else she could possibly say to her mother, Evelyn stuck her head in the door. "Everyone, get out here and help the kids."

The building cleared out, except for Molly's mother, who refused to move. "The kids" turned out to be Hadley and three of her friends who Molly had seen around before. They filed in, hefting a folding cot, tiny wooden table, and cushioned chair.

They stopped in the lobby, set down their loads, and looked around. Mayor Wright squeezed in behind them, pulled the key off the nail and handed it to Hadley, who unlocked the door.

Molly moved to the back of the cell as they arranged the furniture in the small space. They filed out and Stan came in behind them directing Kyle, who was carrying a large cooler. They dumped the cooler in the cell as well.

Just as Molly was beginning to think they were running out of space, Evelyn shuffled in with a pile of pillows and blankets and dropped them on the cot.

Once everything was in there, Mayor Wright elbowed her way through the crowd again. She held a nondescript box, which she dropped in the corner. She stood and stared at Molly. "You won't like that, but it's the best we can do."

The mayor left Molly's cell and shut the barred door behind her. Molly lifted one flap on the box and peeked inside to see a portable potty, complete with a bucket. Oh, good lord.

She dropped the flap and turned to her audience. "Thank you all so much. This is really nice." Molly looked at her mom. "With all this stuff, it beats camping."

"There's lunch and snacks in the cooler," Evelyn said.

"We'll bring dinner tonight, sweetheart," her dad said.

"I got a generator and lights I'll set up," Kyle said.

Mayor Wright placed a hand on Janet's shoulder. "By night-fall, this place will be as nice as any house in Theia."

Molly sat on the cot, the soft folds of the comforter tucked around her. Kyle's generator was loud, but she was thankful for the lights and the phone charger. She was also thankful for the bottle of wine and glasses Etta had left with her before heading to bed.

It wasn't that Etta or her mom weren't willing to sit with her all night. Both had offered, as had her dad and Evelyn. But she'd told them all to leave her. They didn't need to sit on a chair all night, and there was no way another cot would fit in this tiny space. It took a little doing, but she was alone now, sipping wine and reading a romantic suspense novel.

When the door opened, she expected her mother, maybe Etta, perhaps even Kyle, who'd stopped by twice already to make sure the generator was working. But it wasn't any of them.

Seph walked in the door like she owned the place and shut it firmly behind her. She grabbed the key off the nail without any hesitation and walked to the cell. Still silent, and with a look of pure determination on her face, she unlocked the padlock, stuck the key back on the hook, and swung open the cell door.

She eyed the bottle of wine and Etta's glass sitting on top of the cooler for a brief second before she filled the glass nearly to the top and sat down on the cot next to Molly.

Chapter Twenty

"I suppose you want to know—"

Seph held up her free hand. "No. We're not talking about it."

"We're not?"

Seph took a sip of her wine, pulled the glass away, and licked her lips. "No." She leaned back against the brick wall. She jerked forward quickly, grabbed one of the two pillows Evelyn had brought, and shoved it behind her back. "This mattress isn't bad."

"Of course not, it's from the Primrose."

Seph laughed. "That checks out. I suppose your parents brought all this over?"

"Actually, it was half the town. It was a real party. You missed it."

"Mmmm. I did."

Molly waited to see if Seph would volunteer the information she wanted. Where *had* Seph been during that time? When Seph remained quiet, she considered asking directly. But she stopped herself. There was something in the air between them, warning her. "So what are we allowed to talk about?"

Seph waved her free hand. "So many things. Anything. How about your first kiss?"

Molly laughed. "We're sitting in a hundred-and-thirty-year-old jail cell and you want to talk about my first kiss?"

Seph took another sip. "Yep." With a tiny bit left in her glass, she leaned forward, grabbed the bottle and poured herself more before topping off Molly's glass. "First kiss. Go."

"Okay. It was the summer between freshman and sophomore year. I was in a softball league, and it was one of my teammates."

"What was her name?"

"Jenny something."

"Something? Come on. Wasn't her name on her jersey?"

"Right." Molly laughed. "Okay. Let me think about what she looked like from behind." She squeezed her eyes closed.

Seph laughed. "Oh god."

"Okay. I think it was Hernandez."

"Okay. And?"

"It was after a game. We won. And we were at the ice cream place."

"Wait, in Theia?"

"No. I went to school in Bozeman. At my mom's school actually. Anyway, that's the team I was on, and that's where we were when we got ice cream. So this place is at the edge of town and there are woods behind it."

"I can see where this is going."

"Yeah. We went into the woods with our ice creams and ended up making out."

"So first kiss was more than a peck? It was a full-on make-out session?"

"Yeah. Is that weird?"

"I don't know. I mean mine was like a peck, and I thought that was normal."

Molly propped one leg on the cot and angled toward Seph. "Tell me more."

Seph ran one hand through her hair, sipped her wine, and grinned at Molly over the lip of the glass. "Shelly McCabe, sixth grade."

"Oooh. Tell me about Shelly."

"She and I were in the same gymnastics class."

"Gymnastics?" Molly's gaze roamed over Seph. "I can see that."

Seph tapped her tongue on her upper lip. "Yeah. So, one day after class, both of our parents were late picking us up. And we were out in the parking lot alone. And it just sort of happened."

"The peck?"

"Yeah."

"So what was your first kiss that wasn't a peck?"

"Milo Timke. Ninth-grade homecoming dance. It was awful. Very wet and sloppy."

"Hmm. The sloppy kiss. Gross."

"I might have been turned off on kissing altogether if it weren't for this girl at sleep-away camp, Kelly something. She turned the whole thing around for me."

Molly wiggled her brows. "I do love a spicy camp story. Go on."

Seph launched into the story, and Molly settled back on the cot. She'd never dreamed jail could be so enjoyable.

How two women fit on that cot horizontally might be a mystery that would never be solved. But when Molly woke, both she and Seph were crammed onto the slim bed, wrapped together like a cozy burrito. They hadn't turned off the small light outside the cell bars, within Molly's reach, especially since the cell door stood wide open, so it pelted her in the eye as she pried open her lids.

Seph turned and nearly plummeted off the side of the bed. Molly wrapped an arm around her waist and pulled her back. They both made a sound of alarm that ended in laughter as Seph collapsed back against Molly, pinning her to the wall.

"How on earth are we both on this thing?"

"I have no idea, but I'm trapped now."

Seph swung her feet off the side of the cot and sat up, leaving room for Molly to scoot beside her and do the same.

She looked up at Seph. "Good morning."

"Good morning."

"Do you have any idea how or when we fell asleep?"

Seph rubbed her eyes and glanced over at the two empty wine bottles lying on the floor beside the cooler. "No. I blame that."

"You had no idea you'd be spending the night in jail when you woke up yesterday, did you?"

Seph looked at Molly. "I suppose you did."

"I figured I'd be in county lockup, not a scene from Mayberry."

Seph laughed. "I'm pretty sure a call to the state attorney general would turn this circus on its head."

"Don't do that. I realized when they brought in the food and wine that I do *not* want to be in county lockup."

Seph sighed. She gazed at her hands for a long moment. Molly knew she was about to start a conversation neither of them wanted to have.

"I need coffee."

"Me, too."

"And maybe breakfast."

"Yeah. I don't think there's anything left in the cooler."

Seph hopped off the cot. "I'll head to the Primrose and see what I can rustle up."

"Okay. I'll be here."

Seph marched out of the cell and into the small lobby area of the jail, but before she could push open the door to the building, it flew open.

Etta stood on the other side, a tray in one hand and bag in the other, her elbow shoved against the door. "Oh, hey, Seph."

Seph backed into the jailhouse, letting Etta make her way

through the doorway. "Hey. What's up?"

"I brought breakfast." Etta hefted the bag.

Molly clapped her hands. "You're just in time. Seph, you don't have to make the trek now."

Etta moved past Seph with a smile very much plastered on her face, and ducked inside Molly's cell. "There's plenty." She set the coffees and food down on the small table.

Seph didn't join them. Instead, she stayed near the door, her fingers twisting a lock of hair. "I might head back."

Molly cocked her head. "Are you sure?"

"Yeah. I am." Seph sketched a wave then plummeted through the jailhouse door, leaving it open in her wake.

Sun streamed into the little room, hitting the side of Molly's face. The warmth was pleasant, though it was nothing compared to the feel of Seph's body against hers.

"That was weird." Etta plopped into the chair and started unpacking the food. "Why was Seph here so early?"

"She was here late, actually."

"Really? So after you chained yourself to her tool chest and got arrested, she came to see you?"

"Yeah."

"And? Did you resolve things about the Warsaw?"

"Nope. Didn't even talk about it, actually."

Etta shook her head. "I do not understand your relationship."

Molly jolted at the word relationship, but there was no point denying it. That's exactly what they had. "I don't understand it either. But it's happening."

"If we remove the Warsaw from the equation, you seem happy." Etta waved a hand over her. "I mean, here you are, sitting in a century-old jail cell, and you're glowing. Did you have jail sex?"

"We didn't have jail sex. We drank wine and talked and fell asleep." Molly pushed Etta's shoulder. "It's your fault for bringing me two bottles of wine."

"I brought you a red and white so you could choose."

"Well, we chose both."

"I see that. So what did you talk about?"

"Nothing. Everything. Our lives. Basically, everything except Theia."

Etta slung her arm over Molly's shoulders. "You know, I'm probably supposed to say something like you should talk about it, get everything out in the open. Blah, blah, blah. But I'm not. I'm going to tell you that it sounds like you and Seph should keep on avoiding the subject that bothers you so much."

Molly agreed. She couldn't see a way around her clash with Seph over the Warsaw, but she no longer had the will to fight. She wanted more soft kisses and morning cuddles instead.

Chapter Twenty-One

"This has to be the best dinner anyone has ever had in this jail." Molly patted her stomach.

The folding chair Mayor Wright sat in squeaked. "No doubt." The mayor's position on the side of the square card table had her shoved against the wall beside the door. Molly was opposite her, her back to the bars of her cell. The little open area in front of the cells was the only place clear enough of furniture, coolers, and other creature comforts to hold them and Molly's parents for their chicken dinner.

"I'm glad you liked it," her father said.

"It was great, Jeb," her mother said. "And I made cookies." Janet leaned over and slid a box from beneath her chair. Out of it she pulled a handmade basket lined with a red-and-white checkered napkin and filled with three different kinds of cookies.

As soon as she placed it on the table, Molly reached into the basket and plucked out a shortbread round, her favorite. "I'm so spoiled."

Mayor Wright took a sip of coffee, then set the cup on the card table with a muted thump and turned to Molly. "So, now that we all have full bellies, tell me what it is you're trying to get out of this stunt."

Molly took in a deep breath and prepared to lay her practiced speech on the mayor. But she caught her father's eye and let out the breath. She was tired of the speech and all of its carefully crafted reasons. She shrugged. "I don't know. I guess I really wanted people to care about Elise and Bridget."

The card table shifted and squeaked as her father set his elbows on it. "We do. Half the town, including Seph, is involved in finding out more about them."

"It's not just them." Molly ran a hand through her hair. "And maybe it's not about the people who live in this town either."

"What's it about?" the mayor pressed.

"The non-famous people, like Elise, who lived here. I wrote that book about Bub, and everyone loved it. They only read the others because they wanted to get more details on Bub. And as that dropped off, so did readership."

The mayor cocked her head. "So this is about book sales?"

"No!" Molly tempered her volume after the initial shout. "It's about what people care about."

"Okay, I'm sorry. Go on."

"Yes, I'm obsessed with Elise and Bridget. And to tell you the truth, that's what caused me to go down there and chain myself to the toolshed. I realized that Elise and Bridget represent hundreds of forgotten lives."

"So write about them. Write every book in the world. I'll help you promote them."

"What if no one cares?"

"Hmmmmm." The sound came from Molly's mother. It was one of those knowing mom sounds.

Molly stared at her mother. "You might as well tell us what that means."

Janet shrugged. "I think I understand now is all." She flashed Molly a smile that she knew well. There was no way she was getting another word out of her mom on the subject.

Molly clapped her hands. "Okay. Well, thanks to you all for visiting and for bringing dinner." She glanced at the laptop her parents had brought for her today. "I've got writing to do."

Her parents took the hint. They both left their seats and started to pick up the remains of dinner, but Mayor Wright stayed put, scrutinizing Molly from her place across the table.

"Is there something wrong, Mayor?"

"There will be a news crew here tomorrow. Bozeman local news."

Her parents both stopped mid-motion. All three Greens looked at the mayor.

"Yeah. There was a little article in the *Chronicle* about how JP Miller ordered a person to be held in the ancient jail. I've been getting calls."

Janet and Jeb sat back down. Molly placed a hand over her cheek. "I see."

The mayor continued, "Some are from attorneys offering to sue the crap out of JP Miller, the state, the county, everyone. But most people think it's a quaint small-town thing. Anyway, I told all of them that we didn't have any comment, and they'd have to wait until the justice of the peace was back in town."

Molly was grateful. The last thing she planned to do was get anyone else in trouble.

"However . . ." The mayor rubbed her chin. "The television crew is coming whether we cooperate or not. So I decided to play ball."

"You're going to do an interview with them?" Jeb asked.

The mayor nodded. "I would rather direct the narrative than have to react to it."

"I get that," Janet said.

"Me too," Molly said.

"So you're not upset?"

Molly shook her head. "I trust you. You want to protect the town, not to mention JP Miller."

"And you."

Molly swallowed. This was all her fault. She didn't really deserve protecting. "Yeah. Thanks."

"So do you want to be interviewed?"

Molly's brain spun. Her parents and the mayor all looked like they fully expected her to say yes. But Molly wasn't so sure. Since the moment she had marched into the Warsaw, high on her mission to save the back room, things had shifted. Not her need to save the space—that remained the same. The pathway she was on was turning in a new direction.

Being in this jail was no longer about the number of people who might hear her speech. It was about something else, something more tangible. It was about relationships.

Getting herself thrown in a rotting jail brought to the fore-front something she should have known all along, but never quite fully grasped. She had a network, a squad, a family that was much bigger than her and her parents.

Now the notoriety she was originally chasing was bucking up to harm those people. And at the top of that list was Seph. She'd made it clear to Molly, on more than one occasion, that people writing about her or taking her picture or trying to get her to talk on camera during her divorce had left scars. It might not have been the main reason for her flight to Montana, but it was a contributing factor. Molly had never intended to bring any of that down on Seph.

"No, I don't want them in here at all. No pictures of me, no video. Nothing."

Silence blanketed the room. The mayor and her parents all stared at her. Molly caught each of their gazes in turn. Her conviction that she needed to protect Seph was as much a mission of hers now as saving the Warsaw had been when she chained herself to that shed. In truth, it might be more important.

"Okay. What should I say?" Mayor Wright asked.

Molly cleared her throat and scratched her head to buy herself time. It didn't help. She ended up shrugging. "I'm not sure."

Her mother jumped in with a schoolteacher breakdown.

"Okay, let's take this one step at a time. There is an overarching reason for your protest. That's what the press is going to want to know. To make sure that statement fits all the conflicting needs we're experiencing, we should back up and look at all the little pieces that make up the bigger decision."

Janet's hands moved across the table. She was clearly desperate for a whiteboard to sketch this out. Although Molly hated to disappoint her, the process was not necessary.

"I think it's simpler than that. I want to protect the ghost town and bring attention to its historic preservation. Now that I've made my statement about it, I'm satisfied that everyone is working for the best interests of the town. And that's it."

The mayor rubbed her chin. "I think that's a great statement, Molly. Still, they're going to want to know what spurred your protest, or maybe they will already know. The renovations to the Warsaw were mentioned. And there was that viral post from a few weeks ago on social media. It's not a secret."

"So tell them that was the original concern, and it caused me to go off the rails. Now I realize it's all going to be okay."

Her mother tipped her head. "Is that true?"

"That's not the point. It's what we should tell the press."

Mayor Wright pulled herself out of her chair. "Agreed. I'm on it."

"Knock, knock."

Molly laughed as Seph poked her head through the crack in the door. "Why would you say that instead of knocking?"

Seph moved into the jailhouse and shut the door behind her, blocking out the inky black night and moving into the harsh artificial light created by Kyle's generator. "I have no idea. I brought stuff." She hefted a large canvas bag.

From her position perched on the cot, Molly watched Seph

glide through the open cell door with her bulky bag and drop it on the table, which was now back in its spot in the far corner. She stood and joined Seph, peering into it. She ran her hand over Seph's upper arm. "Whatcha got in there?"

Seph pulled out packages of chips and popcorn. "Snacks." Then she gently lifted out a paper bag. "Cookies your father made." A jar came next. It was large and covered with a metal screw cap. The liquid contents were light green. "A mixed drink concoction from Etta." She extracted two clear cups. "Fresh cups to drink said concoction with." Finally, she pulled out a small black box. "And a router."

"A router?"

"Yep." Seph took the box and moved outside the cell. She squatted down near the door, where a set of wires ran through a small hole Kyle had found between the bricks and used to get the energy from the noisy generator outside into the little cell house. "Kyle says this will pick up and recast the Wi-Fi from the courthouse. A repeater, he called it. He was going to install it himself, but he got caught up at the restaurant today. It's crazy out there. The Primrose is full. Tourists everywhere. Anyway, he said this would be simple. I hope he's right."

Seph stood and looked down at the box, now sitting on the floor. A light was blinking. When it stopped, she turned back. "I guess we'll find out."

"Why do I need internet?"

"To watch a movie with me. Duh." Seph plopped down on the cot.

Molly poured the drinks, grabbed the bag of cookies, and sat down beside her. By the time she was settled, Seph had Molly's laptop online. "What should we watch?"

Molly leaned over and nuzzled her nose against the soft skin of Seph's neck. "Something funny. A rom-com maybe?"

"A new one or an old favorite?"

Molly settled back against a pillow and let the warm feeling wash over her. She had never really had this. She'd had lovers, and she'd had friends. No one had ever been both to her. She wanted this every moment of every day. "You pick. I'm game for whatever you want to do."

"I have an old favorite I want to watch with you."

"Let's do it."

Twenty minutes later, Molly finished her drink and reached over to place her hand on Seph's thigh. "I think this movie hits a little too close to home."

Seph pressed pause, pulled the computer off her lap, and turned to look at Molly. "Oh my gosh. The magazine, the evil boss. I'm so sorry."

"I'm not traumatized. It's . . . Wow. I forget sometimes what it was like. Life is different in Theia."

Seph took Molly's hands and held them both in her own lap. "What happened there, Molly?"

Molly let out a long breath. Seph deserved the entire story because it was a big part of what had kept Molly from trusting Seph in the beginning. It was the baggage she'd dragged into the Primrose from that first encounter. It was the start of everything. Molly had to come to grips with it, and she wasn't getting anywhere on her own, so she may as well air it all in front of Seph.

"I started at the magazine fresh out of college. I was so lucky to get that job. It was an assistant job though it was understood that it was a step toward a career. I was so excited. I was the assistant to a lower-level editor named Hannah Killian. I would get up early every day and get to the office an hour before Hannah so I could have everything ready for her. I would stay until after she left, no matter what time it was."

Molly ran her thumb over Seph's knuckles. "After a few years, Hannah left, and I got promoted to be the assistant for the editor-in-chief."

"Kelsy?"

"Yeah. But she's more than the editor. She's the owner of the company. Well, her dad is the owner technically. She's not too much older than us, but her dad basically bought her a magazine so she could have a job."

"Damn."

"Yeah. She was not great at running it. There was a lot of turnover. Probably still is. Anyway, I was clueless about the issues behind the scenes, and I was excited. I did as good a job for Kelsy as I had for Hannah. Better really. I worked my ass off. And it never occurred to me to sleep with my boss, I swear. But I did sleep with a lot of other women at the magazine. And word got back to Kelsy about me."

Seph squeezed her hands. "About your special skills?"

Molly found a way to flash Seph a sly smile through the fog of pain that accompanied this story. "Yeah. Those. So Kelsy came on to me. I went along with it, and we had sex. A lot of it. Constantly, sex. In her office mostly. I became a bit obsessed with her. Or maybe it was the idea of her. I don't really know."

Molly extracted one hand from Seph's hold and ran it through her hair. She had gone over her behavior back then thousands of times. She'd admitted to herself that she had acted like a fool, that she was wrong to have fallen into the trap she did. She could even acknowledge now that she wasn't entirely to blame. Kelsy had been wrong, too. But what she still didn't understand was why it had happened.

Kelsy was not a kind, thoughtful, generous person like Seph. She wasn't compassionate, smart, and funny. She was kind of an asshole. Molly looked over at Seph who was biting her lip in the most adorable way as she waited for Molly's explanation.

"I don't know why I was into her, or why I lost myself so completely in the relationship, or fling, or whatever it was. But I did. So much so that I asked her to date me exclusively. She looked at me like a bug she wanted to squash. I realized in that moment that she had been using me the whole time. I was so angry and hurt I started screaming at her. She screamed back, and then she fired me. Everything I had worked so hard for was gone, just like that." She snapped her fingers.

Seph took the hand she was still holding and brought it to her lips. She gently kissed it. "You were used."

"I was."

"But you picked up the pieces."

Molly swallowed hard. "I did. Theia started out as the place I ran toward to hide. Then I rebuilt myself from the ashes here. I owe everything I am now to Theia. And, this isn't easy to say, but I'm proud of what I made of myself."

A tear dropped from Seph's eye. "You should be."

"I thought I was the only person for whom Theia held magic. I was wrong. It was magical for Elise, too. It changed her life, and Bridget's. And I think I get now it is that for you as well."

There was a beat of time when Seph remained completely still, her hands wrapped around Molly's, her gaze stuck on Molly's face. Then she moved. One hand came up and gripped the back of Molly's head. She pulled Molly into her for a searing kiss.

Several things flew off the cot and onto the wood floor, though Molly couldn't be bothered to care about any of them. She shifted so that Seph was lying beneath her as they devoured one another.

"I need to lock the door." Molly's hand drifted south on Seph's belly even as she said it.

"I locked it with that slider thing when I came in," Seph breathed.

Molly's hand slipped beneath the waistband of Seph's leggings. "Was that because you hoped I would get you naked?"

"Of course."

Molly grinned before plunging back in for more kisses. Her fingers deftly found Seph's clit, and she began to play. Seph ripped her lips away from Molly's and arched her back as a moan escaped her throat.

Molly kissed that long, smooth neck as she worked toward Seph's orgasm. This was what she lived for right here. Seph, strong and agile, purposely giving herself up to Molly, embracing the pleasure Molly could provide, reveling in the feel of Molly's hands and lips. Molly loved to see it, feel it, and hear it. Her own body reacted. The sensation rose as she clamped her thighs around one of Seph's.

Seph dropped her chin, gripped Molly's hair and stared into her eyes. "Yes. Get off, Molly. Do it."

Molly worked them both into a frenzy. Then, in a masterful move, honed from years of practice that now all seemed to have been working toward this moment, she orchestrated a dual orgasm.

They both quivered and cried out. Molly collapsed against the brick wall, wedging herself between it and Seph's body. Seph turned on her side and pressed her head into the hollow of Molly's neck.

For a long moment, the only sound in the room was their heavy breathing until Seph spoke, her voice clear and determined. "Molly. I know our bags aren't unpacked yet. And we're literally in the middle of a giant mess. But I can't deny it anymore. I'm in love with you."

Molly could let fear infiltrate this moment, or she could embrace what she already knew to be true. She took a deep breath. Fear could fuck off. "Me, too."

Chapter Twenty-Two

Something loud woke Molly. A bang perhaps? She sat up quickly, nearly sending Seph flying off the cot.

The sound came again—definitely a thump or a bang. Seph shifted beside her. "What is that?"

When it sounded a third time, Molly realized it was coming from the door. "Someone's trying to get in."

Seph sat up quickly, allowing Molly to get off the cot. She shoved on her shoes and walked through the open cell door toward the heavy wooden door of the jail. Behind her, she could hear Seph shuffling around.

Molly stopped a few inches from the door and listened. A jiggle this time, like someone was determining what mechanism was keeping them out. None of the noises was an actual knock, which is what her parents, or friends, or any resident of Theia, for that matter, would do.

"Is it tourists?" Seph's whisper came from just over Molly's right shoulder.

Molly, not wanting whoever it was to hear, shrugged rather than answer.

The jiggling continued until a recognizable voice shouted, loud and clear, "I said no. Get away from there!"

"The mayor?" Seph asked

"Oh shit. I bet it's the reporter."

"Reporter?"

Molly held a hand over Seph's mouth. "Shh. I don't want them to hear us."

Seph took that hand and pulled it toward her, dragging Molly away from the door. "What is going on?"

"There was an article."

"I know. I got a call from a reporter, which I ignored."

"Well, the mayor didn't. She decided to let them come down because she wants to 'control the narrative.' I told her I would not talk to them. She must have agreed to let them film the outside of the jail."

Seph sank onto the cot. "Ugh. Reporters."

Molly knelt in front of her and placed her hands on Seph's knees. "I'm so sorry."

Seph looked up at her. "Reporters made my life miserable back in San Francisco."

"I know. I'm so sorry."

Seph sighed. "You did what you had to."

"No, I did something stupid. And now it's fucking you up."

Seph gazed into Molly's eyes, not saying anything. Things were so different between them now. Molly felt as though her entire world had shifted. It no longer begrudgingly included Seph and acceptance of their hot sex despite an interpersonal war. Now, in a way, Molly's life had come to revolve around Seph. She wanted to make her come, sure, but she also wanted to make her happy, to see her smile, to hear her laugh, to watch the sparkle in her eye when they discussed the town's history together.

And now Molly was the cause of Seph's current pain She had no idea how to fix it though she desperately wanted to.

"I'll make it right somehow. I'll figure something out."

Seph cupped both of Molly's cheeks. "There's nothing to make right. We are in the situation we're in, and I wouldn't change it."

"You wouldn't change me breaking shit at your saloon and being thrown in jail?"

"Hey, you called it *my* saloon." Seph flashed a massive smile.

"Great. Focus, Seph. You wouldn't change any of that?"

"Nope." She leaned over and kissed Molly. "Because it got us here. I don't know if we could have made it here without your shit."

Molly snorted. "So glad my shit could be useful."

Molly was about to go in for another kiss when there was a proper knock on the door. She stood and approached it slowly, Seph on her heels. There was another knock followed by the mayor's voice. "Molly, it's me. Open up."

Molly unlocked the latch and cracked open the door. The mayor was there, alone.

"I got rid of the reporters. Can I come in?"

Molly and Seph backed into the jail and let the mayor through the door. She relocked the latch and spun around, a look of shock on her face as she examined Seph. "Well, this is a surprise."

Seph sketched a wave, and Molly couldn't help but laugh. "Is it?"

"Maybe not. So what's the scoop? You two decide to stop being enemies and follow your ridiculously obvious sexual tension to its logical conclusion?"

Seph stepped forward so that she stood directly beside Molly. "Yep, that's exactly what happened."

"Well, good. Glad that's settled. Now we have to figure out what to do with these yahoos." The mayor gestured with her hand toward the door behind her.

"What did you tell them so far?" Molly asked.

"I told them that you were an eccentric writer who wanted to bring attention to the needs of the town."

"Did they buy that?"

"Not really. Then I took them to Stan and Kyle and Evelyn,

and they all said the same thing. I think they became frustrated because it's a boring story. They disappeared on me for a minute. Then I found them trying to break in here. Assholes. Anyway, Kyle is escorting them to the restaurant where I'm supposed to meet them to wrap up. No idea what to say." Her gaze flitted between Molly and Seph.

Molly shrugged. "Tell them that's it. No real story here."

The mayor turned her attention to Seph. "Do you think that will work?"

"No idea. They'll make up whatever they want anyway. We can't do much about it. I say show them to the door."

Mayor Wright gave them a firm nod and a smile. "Good. I'll go do that. You all keep the door locked. Nobody needs to walk in on a lovefest in the town jail. They'll wonder what kind of place we have here."

Justice of the Peace Shawn Miller was a tall, slender man who seemed to swim in his black robes. His face was lined with gentle markers of his age. His eyes were soft and understanding. And he smelled like he'd spent hours cleaning fish.

"Well, well, well. Molly Green."

The old town hall, which was originally built as both a courthouse and the center of city government, suited the older man. There hadn't been anything resembling a real trial here since 1905 so, rather than a judge's bench, he sat behind the same long desk the mayor and the rest of the council perched at during their meetings. His hair, still holding the shape of his recently removed cowboy hat, sat over his hawk-like eyes.

"Your honor." Molly straightened her spine. She was alone in the space between the JP and the audience seated in long wooden benches behind her.

"I hear you were causing a ruckus."

Molly schooled her features. She loved the quirkiness of this town, right down to its fishing-obsessed JP who used words like *ruckus*. She cleared her throat. "I was, sir."

"The last time you did that was your junior year of high school. You remember that?"

Molly could feel the heat in her cheeks as she blushed. Most of the people behind her, save maybe Seph and a few others, knew that story yet it was still embarrassing. "Yes, sir. I remember."

"You wanted to make an impression on all your friends at that big city high school."

Molly repressed a laugh at the idea that her Bozeman school, with a total of 1,200 students, was "big city."

"So you threw a bonfire gathering out behind the old general store."

Molly nodded, hoping her acknowledgment would stop him from continuing with the story of her ill-fated teenaged rebellion.

"And those city kids made a big mess, didn't they?"

"Yes, sir."

"And I made you pick it all up."

Molly remembered the weekend spent not only picking up trash, cleaning up graffiti, and tearing down the bonfire remnants, but also cutting the grass, planting flowers, and painting fences.

JP Miller glanced down at a sheet of paper sitting in front of him. "And now you put a hole in a shed with a hammer?" He looked up at her, his gaze piercing. "That is very bad form, young lady."

"I agree."

He raised one eyebrow. "Well, do you have anything to say for yourself?"

"I was wrong."

"That's it."

"Yes, sir."

He scratched his head. "I expected a speech."

"Sorry, sir. I don't have one."

"So if I told you to leave the saloon alone from now on, would you?"

Molly felt exposed. Everyone in the room, except for JP Miller, had heard her rail about the saloon. And now she was backing down, slinking away. She turned her head to scan the crowd. Confusion was the predominant expression on most of the faces that peered back at her.

Then she found Seph, sitting beside her parents, a soft smile on her face. Molly took a deep breath and turned back to the JP. "Yes, sir. You have my word."

"When I spoke to the mayor on the phone, as well as the deputy, it sounded as though you were pretty determined. What changed your mind?"

Molly's entire body tensed as she said something she never in a million years thought she'd admit to anyone, let alone the entire town. "Love."

JP Miller smiled, big laugh lines breaking out on either side of his face. "That, my dear, is an excellent answer. I drop all charges. Go home, Molly."

As soon as the JP left his seat and headed for the door that led to a private office out of sight, the courtroom erupted. Molly's lonely space in the center of the room was flooded with her friends and family. She was caught up in hugs and slaps on the back.

Kyle announced that he was holding a celebratory brunch at the restaurant with free mimosas all around. Molly wanted to be caught up in the joy of this very special community that she was lucky enough to be a part of. But she couldn't fully focus on it because she was searching the crowd for Seph.

Even as they left the courthouse and walked to the restaurant, she couldn't find Seph. At the Oasis, she drank two mimosas and managed to eat a few bites of pastry amid all the conversation. But still no sign of Seph.

Hours later, Molly walked back to the Primrose with her parents and a few guests that had accompanied them to the courthouse that morning. She left them at the front door and headed around the building to the backyard. She wanted to be alone in her cabin. She wanted to call Seph.

But she wouldn't have to call Seph because the woman herself sat on Molly's front porch. Nestled into the wicker chair Janet Green had ordered from an actual, honest-to-goodness catalog, she looked at ease as she watched Molly approach.

Molly waited until she'd come to a stop in front of Seph before she spoke. "Hey."

"Hey."

"You missed the party."

"I was feeling a little emotional and needed a minute." Seph stood and wrapped one arm around Molly's waist. "Are you mad?"

"No, but I'm a couple of mimosas in."

"I'm good with that." Seph leaned in and gave Molly a kiss.

"Do we need to talk?"

"No." Seph ran one hand over Molly's ass. "I don't want to talk. I want to have sex."

"Me, too. But first, you should know that everything I did was out of a misguided sense of self-preservation. And I don't mean preserving the Warsaw or my tours or my books. I don't even mean hoarding Theia for myself because it's my place of serenity. I mean because I was in love with you ten years ago in Berkeley, and I was in love in with you when you barged back into my life two months ago. And I couldn't fathom letting my heart be broken again."

Seph tipped her head. "You were in love with me in Berkeley?"

"I was all in before that party. I was so into you. It was an intense crush. But that night the crush was completely transformed. I know it sounds—"

Seph put one hand over Molly's mouth. "It doesn't sound weird. The morning after our thing in Berkeley, I'm not going to say I was in love with you yet, but I was halfway there. I was totally into finding out where we might go."

Molly kissed Seph's neck. "I don't want to talk about what happened back then."

"Fine, then we won't. We'll talk about what happened here in Theia. Molly, the minute I saw you walk into the Georgette with fire in your eyes and a chip on your shoulder, I wanted you."

Molly ran a finger across Seph's waist and around her belly button. "We should go inside."

"No. Wait." Seph cupped Molly's cheeks in her hands. "You need to know that as good as the sex is—and damn, it is the best ever—my feelings for you go way past that."

"I know."

Seph kissed her gently. "Good. Because I'm not going any-where. I'm not going to hurt you, and I'll chain myself to your cabin to prove it if I have to."

Molly took her hand off Seph to open the door. "We need to go inside and get you naked, right now."

Chapter
Twenty-Three

Molly hit the delete button and watched an entire paragraph disappear. She was at a frustrating moment in time. The book was so close to being complete, but she couldn't quite get there.

It had been a month since her father brought her laptop to the jail, and she'd begun the frantic, obsessive telling of Bridget and Elise's story. She'd learned so much in that time, and her manuscript described every detail.

Elise's family had been traveling all over the American West since the late 1700s. French Canadian fur traders, they were very familiar with the land and the people. Elise's blanket was actually much older than the chest, or even Elise. It was a family heirloom that had been acquired during her grandfather's trading days.

Elise herself grew up on a small farm in Wyoming with eight siblings. She had no interest in the women's work her mother and sister were engaged in. Her father had died when she was young, leaving three brothers to carry on the men's work to support a huge family. So they dressed her in trousers and had her work with them. When she was sixteen, Elise left the farm and wandered to South Dakota. She became Henry and worked as a ranch hand.

Bridget was raised on the family farm, one of five children and the only girl. Her mother died when she was young, though the exact year was lost to history. Much of her childhood was unknown except that she was sixteen when she first met Elise. At some point, Elise told Bridget that she was a woman. And Bridget told Elise that she had always been attracted to women, not men. They'd found each other, and from there a friendship blossomed and love followed.

To be together, they first had to live apart. Bridget would have to stay with her father until Elise could earn the money they needed to run away. And that's where Theia entered the story. The mining town seemed destined to be the beginning of great stories, the cocoon for rebirth, the incubator for love and acceptance. There, Elise, despite being found out by some of the fellow miners, was supported. There she made a fortune that allowed her and Bridget to start a new life.

Molly knew a few things about that new life now, too. She had property records for a sprawling ranch outside of Colorado Springs. It was purchased in 1899 in the name of Henry Dupont. The record indicated that Henry was married.

That was where the story ended. Molly hadn't heard a peep from Marcus about the rest of it. She still didn't know about the baby Bridget was possibly carrying. She didn't know who the strangers were who dropped off the chest in 1971. And she didn't know what, exactly, had happened to Bridget and Elise.

Molly shut her computer and picked up her phone. She texted Marcus. *Hi! Any news on Elise and Bridget?*

It took only a moment for Marcus to respond. *Yeah! Didn't Seph tell you?*

Stunned, Molly frantically tapped the letters. *No. Tell me everything.*

No way. Talk to Seph. She'll want the pleasure of telling you herself. Not taking that away from her!

Molly stared at the phone, open-mouthed. How could Seph do this to her? She pulled up Seph's number and was about to hit the call button when her mood suddenly shifted. She glanced at the clock. Seph was a few hours from the Warsaw's grand opening. She'd laid out her day for Molly that morning over breakfast. She would be swamped right now.

Molly took a deep breath. Her personal emergency did not override Seph's life. She could wait—or she could come up with another plan. That would be the emotionally mature thing to do.

Molly set her phone on the coffee table and reopened her laptop. She could start self-editing the manuscript from the beginning while she patiently waited. She could totally do that. Right?

Molly scrolled to the top of her doc and began reading, or at least she tried. None of the words could penetrate the fog in her brain. She read the same paragraph again and again. Finally, she dropped back, flopping against the couch cushions.

Just as she was about to give up and call Seph, her phone pinged, indicating an incoming text. Molly scooped it up and stared at the screen.

Seph texted, *Hi! Can we meet for lunch today? I have something big to share with you.*

Molly nearly kicked herself for doubting Seph. She immediately texted back, *I'll be there.*

Molly went through the front door of the Oasis. As much as she loved to pop in and say hi to Etta and Rosie, she was too anxious to delay her meeting with Seph today. She was going to get answers, answers that would allow her to finish her book, answers that would complete her own journey to find Elise and Bridget's story.

She spotted Seph in their usual booth at the far end of the restaurant, closest to the door to the bar. She marched in that direction. It was only when she was halfway there that she noticed two people sitting opposite Seph in the booth.

Molly's footsteps slowed as she examined the backs of the heads. One had long brunette hair with flecks of gold that shimmered in the harsh lights overhead. The other had long black braids pulled together with a hair tie at the back of their neck.

Molly slid into the seat beside Seph and held out her hand. "Hi, I'm Molly."

The woman opposite her, with the black hair and deep brown eyes shook it. "Jill."

The other woman took her hand next. Her brunette hair was complemented by bright blue eyes. "Melanie."

Molly glanced at Seph. "Hi."

Seph smiled warmly. "Hi."

"So, what's up?"

Seph gestured to Jill and Melanie. "Molly, meet the great-granddaughters of Elise and Bridget Dupont."

Molly nearly choked on air. "Oh my god. Really?"

Jill grinned. "We are. And we heard you've been looking for us."

"Yes! Oh my god, yes."

Melanie folded her hands on top of the table. "We're cousins. Our mothers were sisters. And they were part of the group of five cousins and siblings that left the chest here over fifty years ago."

"So all those who left that chest were grandchildren of Elise and Bridget?"

"Yes. It was Elise's dying wish," Jill said.

"Elise?"

"Yep. She died at the ripe old age of 101," Jill said. "And she made her grandkids promise to return that chest to Theia. She said she owed Theia. She said it gave her and Great-grandma Bridget a future they could not otherwise have had."

"So, the kids." Molly wiped her brow. The excitement was so great she was literally sweating. "Tell me about them."

Jill and Melanie exchanged a glance before Jill spoke. "Bridget was pregnant when they arrived in Colorado. We don't know how. I mean, no one knows who the father was. That child was born within a month of their arrival. Her name was Hope. A few years later, they adopted four siblings, orphans from the same family."

"So they raised all these kids as a lesbian couple?" Molly asked.

"Yeah. At home at least. All the kids knew they had two moms. But no one outside the family did. When anyone came over, Elise would introduce herself as Henry. That's what the outside world knew her as. Because they lived on a ranch in the middle of nowhere, they could do that. There were some unexpected freedoms back then, I suppose.

"They lived a happy life. At least that's what we've been told. Some challenges, sure. But it was a good life. Bridget died of cancer in 1956. Elise went to live with our grandmother, who was Hope, until her death."

Molly was filled with a strong sensation that she couldn't name if her life depended on it. Then she felt Seph's hand on her thigh, and it had a name. She was in love. And she wanted everyone to feel what she felt, what Bridget and Elise had. The story had a happy ending, which swelled her heart.

Leaving her manuscript had not been easy. Molly was invested in telling the rest of Bridget and Elise's story. Still, she had no choice other than to walk away from her computer tonight.

As Molly and Etta approached the Warsaw, the noise of the crowd that had gathered for this special event penetrated the quiet of the evening. The faint sounds of music underlay the more prominent cacophony of voices all speaking over one another.

"I can't believe how late we are." Etta picked up her stride.

Molly kept up with Etta. She hadn't been late on purpose. She'd been completely wrapped up in her manuscript, and apparently she'd set her alarm for 7:45 a.m. instead of p.m.

She'd nearly jumped out of her skin when Etta pounded on the cabin door at 8:15. Etta had decided that Molly's cargo shorts and "Big Sky, Big Attitude" T-shirt weren't appropriate for the event. Another fifteen minutes of rummaging through Molly's closet followed by a pathetic surrender on Etta's part meant that they ended up leaving Molly's cabin half an hour after the Warsaw's grand opening had started with Molly still wearing the same clothes.

It wasn't a lack of desire to see the final renovations that slowed Molly's steps as they rounded the store and approached the saloon. It was more fear of her own reaction. She hadn't been inside since before she was arrested. She'd told her girlfriend that she didn't want to see her pet project because she wanted it to be a surprise. And that was true. She also didn't want to react poorly and watch Seph's face fall in disappointment.

Now she was on the precipice of seeing the new Warsaw for the first time. She was a few steps away from the swinging pub doors, which had been lovingly restored to their former glory.

Etta looked back at Molly. "Are you coming?"

Molly took in a deep breath and steeled herself. No matter what disappointment lay inside, she would put on a happy face for Seph. She had to.

"Yep." Molly sped up so that she was right behind Etta as she pushed through the doors.

From the moment Molly set foot in the Warsaw it was obvious that the place was alive. And not only with the wall-to-wall crowd of excited patrons. It was brimming with a sense of history in a bright, vibrant way.

Where there had once been decaying wooden floors that only hinted at the hundreds of boots that had traversed them, now there was something much better. The original flooring was still in place, cigarette burns and spur scars intact beneath a thick veneer that showcased and protected the evidence of the Warsaw's first life.

Mayor Wright and Evelyn were entertaining a group of tourists at the bar, which was lovingly restored to look the way it did when Hugh Taft stood behind it. Instead of Hugh, though, Jeff, from the Oasis, was back there, looking dapper in period clothing, and serving up beer and whiskey from glasses that looked identical to the ones in historic photos.

Etta grabbed Molly's hand and pulled her farther into the room. Small round tables skirted a narrow walkway. Molly knew the tables and chairs had been made in a specialty carpenter's shop in Denver, but they looked identical to the ones in the old photos of the Warsaw.

Nearly every chair was filled, and Molly recognized almost every face. She couldn't think of a single town resident, except for the Harmon kids and Patty, their babysitter, who weren't here tonight.

Her parents were in the far corner of the bar, holding court with their guests. Molly stepped closer to see a perfect replica of Bub Roy's poker table. Her father waved at her with a handful of cards.

Molly spun around slowly, taking in every detail, from the saved newspaper clippings lining the wooden walls to the exposed beam ceiling. It was all so perfect. Tears were making their way to the edges of her eyes when she realized that the one person she hadn't yet seen was Seph.

She blinked away the blurriness and scanned the crowd with a new focus this time. Her gaze bounced to each face one by one. But Seph was nowhere to be seen.

A tug on her shirt sleeve had her whirling around to see a grinning Etta. "I found your girl." She pointed toward the back hallway. A small discreet sign with an arrow indicated the restrooms were in that direction. Out of the hallway Seph emerged with Jill and Melanie in tow.

Molly moved toward them instinctively. As she approached, she could see that all three were wiping away tears. Seph's gaze snagged on Molly, and she leaped toward her, catapulting herself into Molly's arms.

Molly wrapped her up and squeezed. Only a few hours had passed since they were last together, but Molly always wanted this. "Hey."

"Hey."

Jill and Melanie both greeted Molly before heading to the bar with Etta. As soon as they were all gone, Seph took Molly's hand and tugged her toward the hallway.

"Are we going to the office for a quickie?" Molly asked.

Seph looked back at her and waggled her eyebrows. "Nope. Better."

"Better than a quickie?"

Molly's stomach clenched as they approached the place where the back room used to be. She wanted to play it cool for Seph, but seeing what had become of Elise and Bridget's special space might be a little more than Molly could handle.

That was exactly where Seph led her. She stopped in front of that fateful door. It was every bit as nondescript as it had been the last time Molly saw it. As plain and ordinary as it was the day Hugh snuck Bridget through it.

Seph opened the door and pulled Molly inside. Molly wanted to close her eyes, but she never got the chance. The small space took her attention from the moment she stepped in. The bare log walls framed the small windowless area. A cot sat along one wall, a thin table opposite it. A ceramic pitcher and basin perched on the table.

And that was it. Simple, small, and exactly as it had been on this very day in 1899. Molly tore her attention from the four walls and the furnishings within and focused on Seph, who stood in front of her with the largest grin Molly had ever seen.

"Oh my god, babe."

Seph placed her hands on Molly's upper arms. "Please tell me you're happy."

A tear spilled onto Molly's cheek. "I'm so happy. So happy. How? How did you do it?"

"I can show you later. We moved the bathrooms to the office and decided to make an annex for that instead. It doesn't matter how. Bryan figured it out. We kept this because it was too important." She moved her hands to Molly's cheeks. "*You're* too important."

"I fucking love you."

Seph kissed her soundly. "Right back at you."

Acknowledgments

This book was a journey for sure. I learned so much writing it, and there are so many people who helped along the way.

This book really starts with my love of ghost towns, nurtured through both the planned and ad hoc exploration of many on my adventures through the Western United States with my partner of twenty-five years. Together we snuck through old, crumbling buildings and wandered lonely dusty streets. Then along came a new companion who shared our love of the campy and creepy. Stephanie catalyzed some of my wildest trips to new and remote places tucked into mountains and perched on tired old ridges.

Theia came to life through my experiences, and Molly, Seph, Elise, and Bridget settled themselves there. I owe my ability to nurture their stories and see them through to the end to many people I've known and loved over the years, but especially to the archivists and museum professionals I've had the pleasure of working with. They showed me the essentials of extracting a story from nothing but paper and rotting wood.

Writing down the arcs of these women and their beloved Theia took some help. I am incredibly grateful to Paula Martinac, my editor. With her expert guidance, I polished this story, letting these gritty, sometimes difficult, women shine in their own unique light. And without the support of Salem West, Ann

McMan, Christel Cogneau, and everyone at Bywater Books, I would not be sitting here writing this acknowledgment to go into this beautifully published and well-cared-for book.

Finally, I have to thank the spectacular K. Aten, who encouraged me to leave behind the ordinary and dive into a career in Sapphic fiction. Without her, I would not have the opportunity to share Theia and her ladies with all of you.

About the Author

Benna Bos has worn more hats than most—and her résumé reads like a Cheesecake Factory menu. She's been a museum director, tour guide, park ranger, college professor, grant writer, and community organizer. And, unsurprisingly, those experiences have a way of finding their way into her novels.

Her true passion, though, is writing. Her debut novel, *Investigating Helen*, won both a Lesfic Bard Award and the Carolyn Readers' Choice Award. She has since written another romantic suspense novel and two cozy mysteries featuring a tenacious basset hound. Her fifth novel, *This Means War*, is a fiery second-chance, enemies-to-lovers romance that weaves together history, conflict, and the undeniable pull between two people who appear worlds apart.

At last, Benna may have found the career that truly fits.

The 2024 Foreword INDIES Publisher of the Year award was presented to Bywater Books for its twenty years of ushering in the "coming of age of queer literature."

"In a year when LGBTQ+ communities faced renewed attacks and the names of DEI efforts were sullied by those in power, Bywater Books remained firm in its commitment to publishing titles that celebrate queer existence and that embrace diversity. Their world-widening books make us laugh, make us cry, and stand as enduring testaments to the breadth of love and the human experience."

–Foreword Reviews

Bywater Books believes that all people have the right to read or not read what they want—and that we are all entitled to make those choices ourselves. But to ensure these freedoms, books and information must remain accessible. Any effort to eliminate or restrict these rights stands in opposition to freedom of choice.

Please join us by opposing book bans and censorship of the LGBTQ+ and BIPOC communities.

At Bywater Books, we are all stories.

For more information about Bywater Books, our publishing mission, authors, and our titles, please visit our website.

https://bywaterbooks.com

www.ingramcontent.com/pod-product-compliance
Lightning Source LLC
Chambersburg PA
CBHW050323110726

47899CB00007B/2344